An Instant Connection

Mike read my mind. "I'm sorry for throwing you in the pool." He looked sincere, but I didn't trust him.

"Good," I said.

Mike's lips quirked. "Friends, then?" He held out his hand.

Mom was watching. "Of course." I bared my teeth so Mike would know I was lying, gave his hand the limpest of clasps, then swept up to my room.

My mom followed me ten minutes later. She looked impatient. "All he did was throw you in the pool. I've seen you push Wendy in lots of times."

She was right, I acknowledged silently. It wasn't getting thrown in the pool that had shaken me— after lying in the sun, the water had been a pleasant shock.

What had rattled me was his kiss.

VIOLET EYES

a novel by

Nicole Luiken

POCKET PULSE

New York London Toronto Sydney Singapore

An *Original* Publication of POCKET BOOKS

 POCKET PULSE, published by
POCKET BOOKS, a division of Simon & Schuster, Inc.
1230 Avenue of the Americas, New York, NY 10020

Copyright © 2001 by Nicole Luiken Humphrey

ISBN: 0-7434-0077-1

First Pocket Pulse printing January 2001

10 9 8 7 6 5 4 3 2 1

POCKET PULSE and colophon are trademarks of Simon & Schuster, Inc.

Front cover montage by Lisa Litwack, front cover photos by Tony Stone Images and Image Bank

Printed in the U.S.A.

For my husband, Aaron,
who doesn't flinch when I ask him
questions about beanstalks
and severed heads.

CHAPTER

1

I HATED MICHAEL VALLANT for nine years before I finally met him.

I had always thought I would recognize him instantly, but I didn't. I was too involved with my own schemes that afternoon down by the river.

It had been my idea to come down to the river in the first place, to beat the muggy August heat by splashing around, but three hours had passed, and the heat had pulled ahead by five points and was winding up for another shot on goal.

Just the way I'd planned it.

When the moment was right, I stood up. "I have an idea. Let's play War."

Maryanne laughed. She thought I was kidding.

Wendy knew better. She grinned evilly. "I'm game. What are the rules, Angel?" Wendy was always up for anything a bit reckless.

The other sunbathing teenagers sat up, looking interested. I was their Idea Girl, the one who could always think of something to do.

"We divide into two teams, the Pirates and the Landlubbers, on either side of the river," I said. "The Pirates try to keep the Landlubbers from reaching the Pirate side of the river with a flag." I looked around for a second, then snatched up the extra T-shirt I'd brought. "This is the flag. Pirates can't come onto the Landlubber side of the river. If a Pirate tags a Landlubber before she crosses the river, the Landlubber becomes a Pirate and tells all the secrets she knows. Everybody got it?"

"Who carries the flag?" Wendy's boyfriend, Carl, asked. A husky blond boy who moved with the slightly stiff movements of a windup toy, his square face held its customary stoic expression. I knew I could count on him to keep things from getting too rowdy.

"That's the secret," I told him.

Nobody else had any questions so we separated into two teams of five people each. "Five minutes to plan strategy and then the war starts," I said.

The Pirates, Carl in the lead, waded across the sluggish brown river. It was quite shallow, thigh-deep in one hollow, knee-deep everywhere else, and dotted with sandbars.

Maryanne, Wendy, and two other girls were on my team. We formed a huddle.

"Who gets the flag? I don't want it." Maryanne nervously tucked a strand of chin-length brown hair back behind her ear.

"Angel," Wendy said. "She's the best runner."

I shook my head. "They'll expect me to have it. You take it. Toss it to someone else if you think they're going to catch you."

We spent another minute discussing strategy before deciding to split up. Maryanne would go downriver, and I would go upriver to draw off the Pirate forces while Wendy zigzagged across and the two other girls tried to protect her.

While Maryanne was doing the countdown Wendy surreptitiously handed me back the flag. She winked at me, and I winked back. Now if the other three were captured and turned into Pirates they would give false information.

"On your mark, get set, go!"

Singing, "Yo-ho-ho and a bottle of rum," Carl's Pirate team splashed into the water, eager to head us off. The current got stronger out toward the middle, and one of the boys was knocked off his feet for a moment. I saw Wendy swerve left around him and heard one of the other girls shout and turn Pirate, but noticed little after that.

I turned and ran upriver. One of the boys, Jimmy, ran parallel to me, ready to cut me off when I tried to cross the river. Carl had obviously assigned each Pirate one Landlubber to watch.

I let Jimmy keep pace close to the Landlubber side of the river until the bridge loomed ahead. The river wasn't very wide, but from the sandy bottom the bridge looked like the feat of engineering it was: three Y-shaped towers cradling a concrete road.

I put on a sudden burst of speed and headed

up the steep grassy bank on my side of the river. Jimmy swore as he realized my intention, and I grinned. I hadn't said you necessarily had to go *through* the river to get to the other side. Since he was so close to the Landlubber bank, he would have to race to beat me back across the river in time to cut me off. Better yet, he would be slowed down by having to check constantly to make sure I didn't double back to trick him. I loved games like this.

A shout from downriver told me Wendy had finally been captured, and now everyone knew I had the flag.

Jimmy would assume that I would cross the bridge using the regular pedestrian sidewalks along the bridge's roadway, but instead I gasped in a lungful of air and headed for the single-lane walkway used by maintenance workers that ran under the bridge.

Halfway to my goal I was forced to break step to avoid colliding with a dark-haired boy. He was a stranger, not part of the game.

He spun around. "What's the rush? Is something on fire?"

"I'm being chased by Pirates," I called back between strides.

"Pirates?" Intrigued, he ran after me, legs flying in time with mine.

"Bloodthirsty Pirates after treasure," I told him.

He drew even. "In that case, would you mind if I joined you?" He didn't even sound out of breath.

I flashed him a grin. "If you can keep up." I poured on the speed. I'd just spent two weeks at a summer volleyball camp with a sadistic coach who made us run five sets of lines a day, and I was in great shape. The wind tore through my short blond hair, and my thigh muscles burned pleasantly.

The boy lengthened his stride, turning the run into a real race. I beat him onto the one-lane hidden walkway by half a step. My footsteps echoed loudly on the planking, but it seemed quite sturdy, and there were handrails on both sides. I kept to the middle and let fly with my elbows to keep him from passing.

I snuck a glance down the river—the view was quite good from this height and not blocked by trees, as it was from above—and saw that everyone was now running toward the Pirate end of the bridge to cut me off except for Maryanne, who seemed to be just sitting on the riverbank, held at bay by one Pirate. Of course, she was also keeping Sean out of the race, so that was okay.

When I was two-thirds of the way across, Wendy gained the bridge. "Avast, me hearties!" she yelled. When Wendy switched loyalties she did it wholeheartedly.

I stopped dead. "Oops."

"Turn around. I'll cover your retreat," the dark-haired boy offered.

"Nah. Jimmy will have cut off the other side." I was trapped. The Landlubbers had lost.

Funny thing, but I had never liked losing. Something reckless surged inside me.

"There's something I forgot to tell you," I said, looking over the railing as Wendy pounded closer. It really was quite a distance down.

Death to fall. The brown water moved hypnotically below, drawing the eye so one unconsciously leaned forward. . . .

"What?" the boy asked.

"We're playing boys versus girls. You're a Pirate." I seized the railing with both hands and flipped over headfirst.

I'd practiced the same move over and over on the uneven bars in gymnastics, so it wasn't *quite* as dangerous as it looked, but I must admit the kaleidoscope of sky and water did look a little scary before my feet landed neatly on the girder I'd spied earlier. Wendy yelled, and guilt pricked my smugness. She and the boy probably thought I'd committed suicide.

He swung his leg over the side and started to follow me. He didn't yell, although he did look a little pale underneath his tan. "Show-off."

I went sideways toward the last Y-support holding up the bridge. Each Y-support had two legs rising out of a concrete base and crossbeams X-ing the two together every three feet. They looked like giant ladders, and I quickly started down. The boy followed.

Hand over hand, strut by strut, he chased me down the giant steps.

"Exactly what is the treasure?" he asked.

My arms and legs moved rhythmically. "A flag."

I hooked my ankles around a horizontal crossbar, let go with my hands, and hung upside down. I took the T-shirt-flag out from under my shirt and threw it into the river, just as the boy slid down a big X and tagged me.

"Too late!" I swung myself up again, untangled my legs, and seated myself comfortably on the bar. Together we watched the current grab the T-shirt and unsnag it from a rock. It had just brushed against the Pirate shore when Wendy's head popped into view above us.

She was gasping for breath. "Angel, you're crazy!" She seemed to notice the boy with me for the first time. "And you're just as nuts as she is."

"Hi," the boy said back.

"Nice of you to drop by," I added.

She glared, but was too busy sucking in air to say anything.

I used the time to take a closer look at my companion. He was around my age, seventeen, maybe a year older, and, in addition to being very fit and tanned, he was extremely good-looking. Thick black hair, straight black brows, a strong jaw, and blue eyes. His nose had a small bump on it, but other than that he was to die for. Very sweaty, but then, so was I. I grinned at him like an idiot. There weren't very many people who could keep up with me.

"Are you going to introduce us?" Wendy demanded as Carl caught up with her. He looked unruffled, as if he could have single-handedly stopped the Iran-Iraq war and finished in time for supper.

"Nope," I said cheerfully. I relented under her stare. "I can't. I don't know his name."

"Ah." Wendy nodded wisely. "You just happened to run into each other *three-quarters of the way up a bridge*." Her voice rose at the end.

I tried to be helpful. "On the riverbank, actually."

Carl saved Wendy from more teeth-gnashing. "I'm Carl Whittier. This is Wendy Lindstrom."

I smiled at the boy. "And I'm Angel Eastland."

"An angel? Now, why didn't I guess that?" His smile was warm and amused and very interested in me. I didn't mind. I was interested right back.

Wendy interrupted our eye-lock. "That's your cue. Now you say, 'My name is . . .' "

"Mike. Michael Vallant."

It was five in the afternoon, and the sun was shining hard enough to require sunblock, glinting off the water, but I felt as if I'd been plunged into an ice bath.

My face stiffened, my smile ironing out. "Vallant? V-a-l-l-a-n-t? *Valiant* with an extra *l* instead of an *i?*" I looked more closely at his eyes. They were violet, not blue, a dead giveaway if I'd been paying attention.

Wendy looked merely curious, Carl calm as always, but something shifted beneath Mike's lazy smile. "Why, yes. Have we met before?"

"No." Flatly.

"Then how come you know how to spell my name? It's rather unusual." He was still smiling pleasantly, but the light flirtation had evaporated.

"I saw it on a trophy."

Before anyone could say another word, I descended rapidly, practically running away, although I never ran from anything.

I was so agitated that I almost forgot the

whole purpose of the game I had instigated: to check out the view of the river that was normally hidden by the next curve in the riverbank.

As I had expected, the river was another dead end.

Michael Vallant.

The name kept whispering through my mind that night, throwing me into turmoil.

Michael Vallant was here. In town.

I punched my pillow and remembered the first time I'd ever heard his name.

I was in first grade at the time, a student of the terrible Miss Dotson. She and I had become enemies on the first day of school when she called me Angela instead of Angel. When I corrected her, she huffed and said she hoped I lived up to my name.

I set out to be a little devil instead. I pretended to snore when she lectured us. I waved my hand wildly in the air, begging to be called on to give the answer—and then said, "Can I go to the bathroom?" I brought frogs to school and shot rubber bands at the ceiling.

On this particular afternoon Miss Dotson had handed around a worksheet with the words, "When I grow up, I want to be a _____." There were pictures of a policewoman, a firefighter, a doctor, a carpenter, and a teacher, and then there was a space for us to draw our own if it wasn't on the list.

She went around the classroom, stopping at each desk, complimenting Ashley on her coloring, correcting Peter's spelling of "movie star," telling Jamie she would have to study hard to become an astronaut . . . until she got to my desk.

"And what do you want to be, Angel?"

"A tree." I showed her the picture I'd drawn.

She laughed. "You can't be a tree. You were supposed to draw what you want to be when you grow up."

"I want to be a tree," I said stubbornly. The tree had been a trick, but I didn't like being laughed at.

"Well, you can't be one," she said crossly.

"Why not?"

"You're a person, not a tree."

"So?"

"So you can't turn into a tree." She was tiring of the game.

"But you told us we could be anything we wanted if we worked hard enough."

She didn't like that reminder. "Don't be difficult. Pick something else." She moved on to examine Davy's scribble.

But I didn't pick something else. I sat there and remembered everything I could about trees. While the other children opened their math workbooks, I cut out paper leaves and put them in my hair. When I stood up I shed them like the fall trees outside.

Miss Dotson took the leaves away from me, but the minute her back was turned I colored my arms and face green with a marker. Bright green. Frog green. When she tried to make me go to the bathroom to wash it off, I clung to my desk with both hands, screaming, "Stop! You'll tear up my roots and kill me! Help!"

For the rest of the day I wilted as if I hadn't been watered, and I refused to answer questions. "Trees don't know math."

At the end of the day, worn to a frazzle, Miss Dotson "transplanted" me to the Quiet Corner. "I swear, Angel, you're almost as bad as Michael Vallant."

If she had meant to intimidate me, she failed. I immediately aspired to behave worse than Michael Vallant. Fortunately for Miss Dotson, halfway through the school year my father got transferred to another town, and we moved.

We moved frequently—five times in the next ten years—and in every town I ever lived in there were signs of Michael Vallant's presence.

Michael Vallant had won every contest and every trophy a year before I did.

"That's a good idea, Angel," my teachers would say, "but Michael Vallant had the same idea, and we did it last year."

"The volleyball team won Zones last year—but of course, we had Michael Vallant on our team then," the coaches would say.

". . . And the winner for the most boxes of chocolate sold is Angel Eastland. Congratulations, Angel. I didn't think anyone would ever touch Michael Vallant's record, but you've come very close."

"I wish Mike hadn't moved away," my girlfriends would sigh. "He was the greatest."

I almost came to hate him.

When I moved to Chinchaga last fall, virtually the first thing I did was examine all the trophies

at school for the telltale brass nameplate. I was
amazed and then overjoyed not to find even one
with Michael Vallant's name on it. No "Most
Valuable Player 1986," no "Curling Championships," no "Intramurals." For once I would
put my name on the trophies first: "Angel
Eastland 1987." When he moved to town after I
left, people would say, "Too bad Angel moved.
She could always come up with great ideas."

It had never occurred to me that we would be
in the same town at the same time.

Because of the eerie way he had always moved
one town ahead of me, I had assumed his dad
must have the same kind of job mine did and that
their employers were rotating them on purpose.

I shivered in my bedroom, under the covers.
It would be all right even if he moved here, I
assured myself. He was a grade ahead of me. We
would avoid each other.

I got my first inkling that things might not be
so simple the next evening at Wendy's house.

Her pregnant stepmother was having a baby
shower, and Wendy claimed she would go nuts
alone listening to a bunch of women ooh and
ahh over fuzzy sleepwear with fuzzy feet. "And
Raven will be so careful not to tear the wrapping paper; she'll fold it all up to reuse it. What's
she going to use it for, I ask you? None of her
friends are pregnant; they've all had their kids."
Resentment shaded Wendy's voice as I followed
her down into the basement den.

Wendy didn't get along with either her stepmother or her father.

Witness our first meeting back in January, when I'd persuaded the entire social studies class to lie about their names to our new teacher. "Then tomorrow answer to your real name, and the next day switch again. By Friday we should have him totally confused, all right?"

"One small problem," Wendy had said, looking cool and tough in a black long-sleeved shirt and acid-wash jeans, her long brown hair stiff with hairspray. "Mr. Lindstrom knows me, so I'll have to go by my real name."

I didn't find out Mr. Lindstrom was her father until two days later, and she never told him about our joke. Her dad still sometimes called me Harriet.

I expected Wendy to ask me why I'd run off the day before, but she only referred to it obliquely. "You should have stayed longer yesterday. We had a marshmallow cook-off to see who could get the best golden tan. Then we did polka dots and stripes. We had a blast."

My stomach tightened. "Whose idea was that?" As if I couldn't guess.

"Mike's. He's cool. Carl asked him to play volleyball with us on Saturday. We're always short a player." Wendy looked at me sideways, but I didn't object.

Inside, my heart sank. In one short evening he'd managed to get in tight with all my friends.

I changed the subject, and we talked about movies and clothes while listening to rock music. Loud rock music. Def Leppard and Bon Jovi. Whitesnake.

"This is the only way to listen to music," Wendy said. "So loud you can feel it vibrate in your chest."

Just before eight, when the guests were scheduled to arrive, Mr. Lindstrom came downstairs and asked Wendy to turn the music down.

"What?" Wendy pretended not to hear.

"Turn it down!"

She turned it down one notch.

He winced. "More."

She turned it down two more notches. "How's that?"

"All right," he said grudgingly, and started back up the stairs.

"Wouldn't want to disturb the unborn child," Wendy said softly.

He paused at the top, a slim, neatly dressed man with thinning hair. He looked oddly helpless. "I don't understand how you can listen to this stuff. You used to love classical music. How come you never play the piano anymore?"

"I have a tin ear," Wendy said.

"You were so good at it."

"Sometimes we outgrow things," she said between clenched teeth.

He just shook his head and left.

Wendy hugged her elbows, staring straight ahead. "He doesn't listen. I've told him a hundred times I'll never play the piano again."

For the first time, I noticed the piano in the corner of the room. Wendy had done her best to bury it under stacks of paper and some clothes.

I risked a question. "Were you a child prodigy or something?"

"You'd think so, but no. I just took some piano lessons as a kid." Wendy clearly didn't want to talk about it. "Which movie do you want to watch first? *Police Academy 3* or *Top Gun?*" She held up the two tapes.

I voted for *Top Gun* even though we'd already seen it once before, and we drooled over Tom Cruise. Wendy had provisioned the den with soda pop and chips, so we didn't poke our heads upstairs all evening.

Raven called down for us to go to sleep at one o'clock. We broke out the sleeping bags but continued to talk for an hour.

Just before we dropped off to sleep, Wendy mentioned Mike again. "He was asking about you. Did you know him Before?" She laughed. "Or should I say After? Get it?"

I didn't get it, and my heart began to pound against my rib cage. "What do you mean?"

But Wendy was through being indiscreet. She looked at me in admiration. "You never slip, do you? I catch myself half a dozen times a day about to say the wrong thing, but you never slip. It's disgusting. I'd better go to sleep before I cost Dad a thousand bucks. Good night." She turned over and slid straight into dreamland.

I lay awake half the night, staring at the ceiling, trying to figure out what she had meant. I felt chilled, as if I had touched the tip of an iceberg but had not yet begun to comprehend the vast, dim shape below.

CHAPTER

2

I DREAMED OF CHOKING SMOKE and twisting orange flames. Flames that roared, taller than my head, taller than the ceiling. I was small, crawling on hands and knees like a mouse chased by a cat, searching for a bolt hole. But the fire cut me off, climbing the curtains and ringing the window. Burning timbers fell from the ceiling, and I screamed, trapped. As the ferocious heat of the blaze began to singe my hair, I squeezed my eyes shut.

Fire painted the inside of my eyelids—

I jerked awake and found myself still in Wendy's basement. No smoke, no fire, just a fluorescent light overhead that all but blinded me. I rolled over and tried not to shake with relief. It was just a dream. An old dream, at that. An old memory.

"It's eight o'clock," Raven said. She was standing at the top of the stairs. Heartlessly, she turned on the rest of the lights. She was a tiny, exotic-looking woman with dark hair and high cheekbones. Wendy had once told me she had the blood of Indian princesses in her veins. I could almost believe it. Raven had an inborn serenity that made me think of royalty.

When Wendy pulled a pillow over her head and grumbled that it was too early to get up, Raven calmly reminded her that Carl was coming to pick her up at eight-thirty.

Wendy gave a shriek worthy of a scalded cat and leaped out of bed. "I haven't even taken a shower yet."

Raven looked amused. "Don't worry. I told him to give you an hour."

"You told him?" Wendy raised an eyebrow in disbelief. "You actually spoke to him on the phone?"

For reasons that baffled me, Wendy's parents didn't approve of Carl.

"Yes," Raven said evenly.

Wendy nodded. "Of course. If you hadn't told him, he would be sitting in your driveway for half an hour." She headed for the bathroom, and Raven went away.

We each took a shower, then shared the tiny bathroom to do our hair and makeup. It took me ten minutes to blow-dry my hair and put on a touch of eye shadow and blush.

Wendy carefully outlined her left eye with black eyeliner and mock-glared at me. "How can you be done already? I still look like I've been hit by a tornado."

Wendy had twice as much hair to style as I did, and her recent perm had left her with a tangled mess of corkscrew curls, but I struck a pose and said, "It's because I'm perfect and you're not."

She laughed. "Well, that's true. We mortals can't be expected to compete with goddesses like you."

Her remark disturbed me. "I'm hardly a goddess."

"Next thing to it. Blond hair, violet eyes, skinny. You've got all the boys panting after you."

"Not all of them."

"Name one."

"Carl." His loyalty to Wendy was legendary.

"That's different," Wendy said, without explaining why. "Name another one."

"Sean, then," I named my ex-boyfriend. We had had a particularly messy breakup a month ago.

"Ha. Sean had the biggest crush on you of the lot. Why do you think he acted like such a jerk when you two stopped dating?"

I hadn't thought of it quite that way. "Jimmy." Everyone knew he liked Maryanne.

"Only because you've never paid any attention to him. He was sweet on you back in January. If you smiled he'd switch loyalties in a minute."

"You're exaggerating," I said, a little more sharply than I'd intended.

She shrugged. "Not really. You could be a

movie star if you wanted to. You naturally attract people. Even Mike. You snubbed him horribly yesterday, and he was still asking about you."

I did not want to hear about Mike. "I'm hungry. Are you almost done?"

Wendy gave her stiffened bangs one more backcomb, then nodded. "Let's go."

If I'd been voting on the most perfect person, I would have voted for Raven. My mother would have let us fend for ourselves with toast and cereal. On a special occasion she might have made bacon and scrambled eggs. Raven had set out cloth napkins and cutlery that matched. Golden waffles steamed on a china plate, and fresh fruit brightened a crystal bowl. The sun shone in through the kitchen window, and all the white counters and cupboards gleamed.

Wendy's jaw set. "I told you not to go to all this trouble."

"I enjoyed it," Raven said mildly. "Besides it wasn't all for you. Your father and I already ate. He had a golf game." School would begin next week, and Mr. Lindstrom would soon have to give up his early morning games.

I dug in. The food tasted delicious, and I said so. Raven nodded serenely from her rocking chair in the corner of the living room. The turquoise baby blanket she was crocheting frothed over her lap.

"What are you going to do today?" Wendy scowled suspiciously.

"I thought I'd do the laundry," Raven said, unruffled.

"I'll go get my hamper." Wendy stomped downstairs.

Raven stared after her a moment, yarn wrapped around her fingers. "I don't understand that girl. She's furious at her father about the baby, but ever since she found out I'm pregnant she won't let me do any hard work. She does all the vacuuming, all the hauling things up and down stairs, and all without my saying a word. I turn around and it's done. Every time I sit down to supper she's poured me a glass of milk, and when I was having morning sickness she did all the shopping and cooking. Yet she isn't any friendlier. We aren't any closer." She sighed.

"How long have you and Mr. Lindstrom been married?" I called Raven by her first name, but because he was my teacher I had trouble thinking of Mr. Lindstrom as Don.

"Six years, but Wendy's been living with us only for the last four."

I wanted to ask where Wendy had lived before that—I'd never heard her so much as mention her real mother—but just then she came back up the stairs, hauling a basket of dirty clothes. She vanished into the laundry room, and we heard the sound of a load being put in the washer. I was starting to see what Raven meant.

The doorbell rang, and Wendy ran to get it. "That'll be Carl."

"Of course." Raven looked pointedly at the clock. It was exactly nine o'clock. Carl was never early or late, always on time.

I got up to follow Wendy, but Raven stopped me. "You seem like a nice girl, Angel." She pronounced my name with an odd accent. "Wendy's father and I are concerned about her . . . attachment to the boy."

"Boy?" I forced her to say the name.

"Carl. We would appreciate your help." She didn't say it directly, but she wanted to break them up.

The half-liking I had been feeling for her slithered down the drain. I could have told her the same thing I had told Mr. Lindstrom, that Carl was the best thing that had ever happened to his daughter and that I was a far more dangerous companion to her—Carl would never have pulled the stunt I had on the bridge. Instead, I just said, "I like Carl," and left it at that.

"If you truly like him, you will help me. Wendy is no more good for him than he is good for her. She's only dating him to rub it in her father's face. The situation is dangerous." Raven's voice was low and serious.

Dangerous?

"No." I went down the hall and found Wendy waiting for me at the door. She was tying her shoes, and I couldn't see her expression, but I felt a slam of fear. Had she heard me talking to Raven?

Wendy's relationship with her parents was fragile enough as it was—I didn't want to damage it unduly—but at the same time, if Wendy had heard, I couldn't risk not telling her.

It was a bitter thing, but even if I hadn't liked Wendy—and I did like her, a lot: her cynical

sense of humor, her wildness, her absolute loyalty to her friends—we would still have been
best friends. Because Wendy was sometimes
indiscreet. Her tongue slipped, and I got hints of
puzzles within puzzles as I had last night. I
needed her information, so while we were walking to Carl's pickup truck I said, "Well, that was
interesting. Your stepmother just tried to enlist
me to her cause."

Wendy's shoulders relaxed infinitesimally
inside her red windbreaker. She had heard. "Oh,
yeah? What did you tell her?"

"That Carl was nice."

"He is," Wendy said softly. We'd reached the
pickup. "Don't tell him, okay?"

I mimed zipping my lips together, something
that always cracked Wendy up. They must not
have done that at her elementary school.

Laughing, Wendy climbed into the pickup
truck and scooted over close to Carl. She gave
him a slow kiss on the lips.

He didn't smile—he did so rarely—but his gaze
was tender, and his hand covered hers for a
moment before he shifted the truck into reverse
and backed down the driveway. His movements
held a calm deliberation that I found soothing.
Carl could never be accused of being chatty, but
when he did say something it was usually worth
listening to. His observations were concise and to
the point. I often thought he was Wendy's rock,
her anchor in the wild sea of her recklessness.

Mr. Lindstrom referred to Carl as "that damn
robot." If someone talked to me like that I

wouldn't be too eager to pin my heart on my sleeve either.

When Carl and Wendy had first started dating five months ago, a buzz had gone through the entire school. Maryanne had whispered the news to me as if it were a scandal. I hadn't understood it then, and I didn't understand it now. The rank prejudice smelled of racism, but Carl was blond and blue-eyed with lighter skin than Wendy, and nobody had so much as blinked when Sean and I dated, and his parents had immigrated from Jamaica.

"Are you sure you don't want to come, Angel?" Carl asked me as he slowed to a stop in front of my house. Raven probably thought we were all going to the movies together, but I wasn't dating anyone at the moment and would have felt like the odd man out.

"Positive. All I want to do today is laze around by the pool and improve my tan." A small lie. I fully intended to swim some lengths first.

"All right," Carl said, but there was a tiny crease in his forehead—the equivalent of a frown from anyone else. I remembered that he, too, had seen my odd reaction to Michael Vallant, and I was touched by his concern.

"See you Saturday," I said cheerfully, before hopping out of the pickup. Saturday was the second-last day of summer vacation, and our group had a big party planned.

Inside the house, I found Mom in the living room, with her blond hair tied back in a bright yellow scarf and newspapers all over the floor.

She was taking a class in watercolors and was trying her hand at painting.

I studied the greenish blue blobs on the easel. They were either turtles in an ocean or green spaceships in a speckled sky.

"What do you think?" Mom asked cheerfully. "Should Picasso be shaking in his shoes?"

"I don't think Picasso did watercolors," I said. Our eyes met, and we snickered together.

"Oh, well," Mom said, "I'm having fun. Do you have any plans for today?"

"I thought I'd head over to the pool this afternoon."

"Can you pick up some green onions for supper? We're having company."

"No problem."

The pool was full of little kids splashing around when I arrived, so I decided to save the laps for later and sprawled out on one of the lounge chairs. I let the sun soak into my skin and tried, unsuccessfully, not to think about Michael Vallant.

I had just gotten relaxed when a shadow fell over me.

"Would you mind moving? You're blocking the sun." I didn't look up.

"Why go to the pool if you're not going to swim?"

I recognized the voice. Fortunately, my sunglasses hid my reaction to Mike's appearance. "To tan. The sun reflects off the water, and you tan faster," I explained slowly as if to an idiot. I flipped over onto my side, ignoring him.

He didn't like that. Probably not very many girls had ever ignored him.

"So what you're saying is that the closer you get to the water the better your tan?" he asked.

"Give the man a prize."

Quick as a cat, he scooped me up in his arms. I'm five feet six, not exactly petite, and I'd never been carried by a guy before. The shock of it blunted my reactions for a precious second.

"What are you *doing?*"

"Just trying to be helpful," he said blandly and kept walking.

"Let me go!" I hit his chest with the heel of my hand.

"Okay."

At the last second I realized he was holding me over the water, and I grabbed furiously, trying to get a lock on his wrist so I could drag him in with me. He slipped free, but I twisted while falling and grazed my head painfully on the side of the pool.

I let myself slip down into the water, limp, trailing bubbles, then slowly bob back up in a perfect dead man's float. I was on the swimming team and could hold my breath for close to two minutes.

I felt a splash beside me, and Mike grasped me under the arms and towed me back to the edge of the pool in a perfect lifeguard's hold.

While he was hauling me out, I stole two shallow breaths, but stayed perfectly limp. He positioned me on my back on the tile, but instead of calling the lifeguard he tipped my head back. Air passageway open. Then he pinched my nose closed and began performing mouth-to-mouth resuscitation.

A very strange form of resuscitation, I realized, as his lips shaped mine. More like a kiss.

He knew I was faking!

I almost jackknifed upright at the realization but managed to turn it into a weak cough instead. I rolled onto my side and heaved in several breaths just as two lifeguards dashed over.

"Is she okay? What happened?"

"I'm fine," I said weakly, and coughed again.

Someone crouched by my side. The devil himself. "Are you sure you're all right, Angel? You scared the hell out of me." Mike's voice was perfect, rough and concerned, but his eyes held unholy glee.

It made me want to kick him.

"You—you dropped me." My voice quavered.

Our audience thought I was being a tad ungrateful. "He saved your life," someone said.

"Did he?" I smiled bravely. "I don't know how I'll ever repay you." *I'll pay you back for this if it's the last thing I do.*

Mike caught the unspoken message loud and clear, but he just grinned.

I accepted a lifeguard's help up. "I want to go home now."

Both the lifeguards were male, so an older woman with two kids went into the dressing room with me to make sure I didn't faint.

I took an extra-long time washing my hair to

make sure Mike wouldn't hang around waiting for me outside, thanked the lady, and then climbed on my bike.

I pedaled home furiously. I was mad at myself for pulling such a juvenile stunt. I'd wanted to get back at Mike for his trick, but I hadn't meant to worry anyone else. *Stupid, stupid.* But mostly I was mad at Mike for seeing through my ruse so easily. Every time I thought about the way he'd kissed me, a red wave of fury and embarrassment rushed through me.

The only good thing about it was that from now on I wouldn't have to just pretend he was my enemy. Now he really was.

Two blocks from home I remembered the green onions and had to go back for them.

I was sweaty, hot, and mad when I finally arrived home. I heard Mom laugh as I went in the door and swung around to the kitchen to drop off the onions.

When I got there my jaw dropped open. Sitting in one of the kitchen chairs, laughing with my mother, was Mike.

"What are *you* doing here?" I spoke without thinking.

Mom frowned at my tone.

"I came here to apologize," Mike said.

Apologize, my foot. "I meant, how did you know where I lived?" And could I move somewhere else?

Mom spoke up unexpectedly. "Your father and Mr. Vallant work together. I've invited the Vallants to supper this evening. Mike came over a little early when he realized you were the one he'd run into at the pool."

My back prickled, and I glared at Mike. Exactly what had he told my mother about what happened at the pool? That I'd almost drowned or that I'd pretended to drown? I didn't know which would be worse.

Mike read my mind. "I'm sorry for throwing you in the pool." He looked sincere, but I didn't trust him.

"Good," I said.

"Angel!" Mom seemed to be expecting something more.

"Apology accepted. And I apologize for calling you a brainless turd."

Mike's lips quirked. "Friends, then?" He held out his hand.

Mom was watching. "Of course." I bared my teeth so Mike would know I was lying, gave his hand the limpest of clasps, then swept up to my room.

My mom followed me ten minutes later. "You weren't very gracious."

"You weren't there," I said shortly.

She looked impatient. "All he did was throw you in the pool. I've seen you push Wendy in lots of times."

She was right, I acknowledged silently, after she finished lecturing me on behaving myself that evening. It wasn't getting thrown in the pool that had shaken me—after lying in the sun, the water had been a pleasant shock.

What had rattled me was his kiss.

CHAPTER

3

DINNER THAT NIGHT signaled the start of the undeclared little war between Mike and me.

We eyed each other warily while the four adults had cocktails; we searched for weaknesses over the boeuf au jus and were needling each other openly by dessert.

"I can smell your perfume. What is it? Chlorine Green?" He kept his tone low and pleasant, to fool the adults at the other end of the table.

"Your nose hairs are blocking your sense of smell. I have some tweezers I can lend you," I murmured back.

I was so wrapped up in scoring points off Mike and avoiding his thrusts that I didn't notice right away what was happening with our parents.

I hadn't taken to either of Mike's parents right off the bat. Mr. Vallant—"Call me Drake," he'd

said with a camera-perfect smile—was handsome but too slick.

He'd brought champagne for some incompre-
hensible reason and insisted on opening it with
a flourish. He had raised his glass in the direction of my mother. "To our beautiful hostess."

Mrs. Vallant was a plump woman who thought
she was thin. Her skirt was too tight and too
short, and she was overdressed for a simple dinner at home. She was still very pretty, and might
once have been gorgeous, but her pout ruined any
lingering beauty. Beside her, my mother's fresh
prettiness shone.

Mrs. Vallant's girlish giggle annoyed me. "I've
got bubbles up my nose. Oops! There goes another
one." She seemed to think this the height of wit.

Drake regarded her with a thinly veiled contempt that only made her try harder. He concentrated all his charm on my mother, raving over
the meal.

"Oh, no," Mom said, flustered and pleased.
"Really, it's just roast beef and mashed potatoes
with a French name."

"It's wonderful," Drake said, still fawning.

Whenever my dad tried to change the subject
by asking him something about work, Drake cut
him off. "No office talk here, Neddy! Tell me, are
there any decent golf courses around here?"

"Well, there's the one—"

"Of course, you have to go to the city to find a
really challenging course," Mr. Vallant interrupted disparagingly. "With my handicap, country golf courses are too simple."

Dad nodded, but I could tell he was bored. He tried to exchange a can-you-believe-this? look with Mom, but she wasn't watching. She was actually laughing at Drake's bragging.

Mike saw my glance. "Better watch out," he said sotto voce. "My father's quite a ladies' man."

"If you like golf bums," I hissed back.

My dad and Mrs. Vallant grew ever more silent as the evening progressed, although Mom and Drake were having a ball. All in all, it ranked up there in uncomfortable meals with the time Uncle Albert and Aunt Patty came to dinner and Uncle Albert complained vocally about the burned chicken my mother had made. I was very relieved when the Vallants finally went home.

On Saturday I caught myself debating whether or not I should go to the party, since Carl had invited Mike. That made me furious because the gang had been my friends first. I went, in the end, and was very glad, since Mike didn't show up.

Maryanne watched for his car all evening and confessed that she "liked him." I held my tongue with an act of will. Everybody else seemed favorably impressed with him.

I didn't see Mike again until the first day of school. We opened up hostilities in the hallway before homeroom, where I had been talking with Maryanne. "Well, if it isn't the boy wonder in the flesh."

"Good morning to you, too, Angel. Stomped on any kittens yet today?"

"No, but there's a slug on the bottom of my shoe. Excuse me while I go scrape it off." I strode off down the hall.

After a few paralyzed seconds Maryanne followed me to my locker. She was gaping, and I realized that until now Wendy and Carl were the only ones who'd seen Mike and me together. "I take it you two don't get along?"

"No." I smiled tightly as I dialed the combination and opened my locker. "I just don't think he's the Superman the rest of you do. Do you mind?"

Maryanne looked puzzled, but also a little relieved. "Oh, well. Less competition."

I laughed. Every time I wrote Maryanne off as a total scatterbrain she came up with something as pragmatic as that.

Mike was a grade ahead of me, so we shared few classes. Unfortunately, because of the small student population of Chinchaga High School there weren't enough students to make a full class unless all three grades were pooled for some electives. My Drama 20 class included Drama 10 and Drama 30 students, and it was the same for phys ed. (Phys Ed 10 was compulsory, but Phys Ed 20 and 30 were electives and ran together.) Mike was in both my drama and phys ed classes.

In phys ed our new teacher, Mr. Hrudey, broke tradition and started us off playing round-robin badminton instead of volleyball.

Because the gym was only big enough for three singles matches to be played at once I sat out the first two rounds and got a chance to see Mike in action.

He was as depressingly good as all the trophies had led me to believe. He whomped Wendy without trouble. Wendy liked to push herself, and she wasn't afraid to sweat, but she always played as if she were hitting tennis balls instead of light, rubber-tipped birdies, swinging her whole arm and forgetting to flick her wrist.

Then Mike sat out while I played my first match against Maryanne. She was a mediocre player at best. Of the four badminton shots she could only do clears consistently. She'd never mastered smashes, and her drops and drives were accidental instead of strategic. It took effort, but I managed to flub a few easy shots and coasted through to a mere 11–9 victory. I didn't want Mike to know the extent of my skill.

I played Carl next, and he was a little harder. Unlike most competitors he gave nothing away with his body language. I never knew which way he planned to leap, so I couldn't place my shots accordingly. He had a powerful arm and could smash birdies like missiles, but he had no sense of strategy. I let him win 15–11. (For some chauvinistic reason women's singles went to 11 points, while men's and mixed went to 15 points.)

I sat another one out and then faced Mike. I could tell from the anticipation on his face that he had fallen for my little act. He thought he could beat me—no problem. He gave up first service without even spinning the racket. "Go ahead and serve. I—"

I gave him my drive serve, fast and mean,

straight at his face. He flinched and missed. One point for me.

"I'm sorry," I said with false contrition. "Shall I re-serve?"

"No, that's all right." Mike scooped the birdie back up at me. I served again, weakly, pretending the drive had been a fluke. Service went to him, and he scored. We traded points for several rounds, his points all falling through blatant holes in my defense, while mine were little dribblers that shouldn't have made it over the net but did, or shots that looked as if they would fall out of bounds but didn't. He looked frustrated but still seemed confident of his skill.

When I pulled ahead 7–6 I suddenly changed tactics, catching Mike by surprise. I wound up my arm as if to do a high, arcing, clear but pulled back at the last second so that the birdie dropped suddenly at the front of the court instead. My smashes gained power, and the weak backhand I'd been feigning disappeared. *Wham! Wham! Wham!* I was up three points before he realized he'd been tricked.

He rallied and got another point back, making it 10–7. After that we both played relentlessly, smashing the shuttlecock back and forth, forcing each other to run to all corners of the court, sliding shots along the net, and trading point for point. Mike returned several spectacular backhand clears—the hardest shot of all—but they only set me up for my point. We were equals on the court, but his earlier overconfidence cost him, and I won 15–13.

"Nice game," Mike said as we shook hands over the net. "Too bad you don't have the stamina to keep it up."

I was so furious I spotted my next opponent five points. My next game happened to be against my ex-boyfriend, Sean, and my words wiped the easy smile right off his face. He was almost a foot taller than I was and in pretty good shape from playing softball. He looked offended. "No."

"Okay," I said. "Ten points, then." I served before he could protest again.

I won 15–10.

I rather regretted spotting Sean the points when I saw the tight look on his face afterward. "Congratulations, Angel." He stalked off the court and threw his racket in the corner.

I swore mentally. I shouldn't have stomped on his pride quite so hard. If Wendy had been right about Sean still liking me, I'd certainly cured him of it now.

In spite of his temper, Sean was a nice guy: good sense of humor, a bit of a flirt, and a wonderful dancer. I felt bad about the way we'd broken up. I had the terrible suspicion I'd hurt him, and I hadn't meant to. I hadn't broken things off with him because of anything he'd done or because I'd liked someone else. It was simply my policy not to date any boy for longer than a month.

Then I saw the ecstatic expression on Coach Hrudey's face and forgot about Sean.

"What a great team!" Coach raved. "Mike, Angel, I'm matching you up for mixed doubles."

For once Mike and I were in complete agreement. "No!"

But Coach ignored our arguments, and I soon found myself standing on the same side of the net as Mike.

I was determined to lose, and so was Mike. We were terrible together. We ran into each other, whacked each other with our metal rackets, and allowed shots to the middle of the court to fall between us without moving a muscle to try to reach them.

Coach Hrudey called a halt to the farce in midgame. "What are you doing?" His thick hands squeezed air. "You're being beaten by Wendy and Maryanne, for heaven's sake. The same Wendy and Maryanne you slaughtered separately."

"We don't mesh together," I said.

"Maybe you should put us on different teams," Mike added.

Coach looked up, blue eyes shrewd. "You're not working as a team. Get back on the court. The next one of you to fumble an easy shot crab-walks around the gym."

He could hardly have come up with a better punishment. I could have borne laps, but not crawling around on my back while Mike looked on and laughed.

This time not a single shot got through our defense. We recovered our deficit and pulled into the lead, winning easily.

"That's more like it." Coach nodded in approval.

Mike and I exchanged looks. I read my thought on his face. I did not want to be paired with him, but at the same time I was determined not to give in first.

The issue was still unresolved when I got home that afternoon. I had the house to myself, a rarity.

It was very quiet. I could hear someone in the neighborhood mowing the lawn. A couple of kids rattled by on bikes. The refrigerator hummed.

I turned on the TV just to make some noise. CBC was still discussing the recent Meech Lake Accord, so I switched to Edmonton's ITV. I lounged back on the couch, alternately crunching on an apple and helping the contestants question the *Jeopardy* answer, but it was an act for a hidden audience.

I couldn't shake the creepy feeling that someone was watching me.

Which, of course, someone was. I just didn't notice it as much when Mom and Dad were home.

Mom came home at five, just a few minutes before Dad got home from work. She whipped off her sunglasses and went straight to work chopping carrots in the kitchen.

Dad arrived and kissed her on the cheek. "Where were you at four? I called to tell you I'd be a little late."

She didn't meet his eyes. "Out shopping."

Dad nodded, but I remembered that Mom hadn't been carrying any bags.

I was only puzzled then, but twice more in the next two weeks she came home after I did, her head down, but her cheeks flushed with high color. Dad stopped teasing her and started frowning. Despite my efforts, supper conversation dragged.

I didn't get really worried, however, until the afternoon a few of us went downtown to play pool during our noon hour. Mike was beating the pants off Maryanne, but she didn't seem to mind as she flirted with him. I was psyching myself up for a grudge match when I happened to look out the window and see my mother getting into someone's car—some *man's* car. A sporty white BMW, not the blue Plymouth my dad drove.

She was laughing, and she looked very young.

I felt as if someone had plunged a knife into my chest.

How could she? How could she do this to Dad and me?

I had caught a glimpse of the man's dark head and recognized him. It was Mr. Vallant.

I turned quickly to see if Mike had seen, but he was concentrating on his shot, smoothly sinking both the one ball and the five ball. Of course, he might have seen this kind of thing before. *"My father's quite a ladies' man."*

Mike was something of a ladies' man himself. He was flirting with Maryanne now, and Maryanne had told me he'd asked Belinda Potter out to a movie last weekend.

I thought about asking Mike to help me break our parents up. Between the two of us we could come up with something. But no. Mike and I were enemies. I had to remember that. There might be an innocent reason for Mr. Vallant and my mother to be driving together, but Mike would always be my enemy, my competitor.

We were still partners on the badminton court, still holding to the truce imposed on us by Coach Hrudey, but that only meant we'd gotten sneakier about continuing our war. When I returned our opponents' shots, it wasn't with the aim of scoring a point, but to set them up to shoot a real zinger at Mike. He did three spectacular saves in one game before he caught on and started doing the same thing to me.

Off the court, we played tricks.

Mike conned my mother into giving him a particularly ugly picture of me as a five-year-old playing in the mud and had it printed in the school newspaper with the caption "Your halo's slipping."

I put mustard in his milk shake.

He stole my sports bra from my gym locker and hoisted it up the flagpole.

I retaliated by getting him a date with not one, not two, but three different girls on the same night.

I'd been expecting a kamikaze attack, so I was puzzled when Mrs. Jamison, our new English teacher, pulled me aside and made me read a page from a John Steinbeck novel. When I finished, she was frowning. "So you *can* read. In that case, what's the meaning of this?"

She handed me a story entitled "The Two Feerless Kitins Have an Adventur" by Angel Eastland.

When I explained that a classmate must have substituted the story for my own creative writing assignment I pretended to be furious, but I later laughed myself sick reading it in the washroom. The story was full of sentences like "the pore little kitin cryed all nite and dint leave the hows" and "Johnny pulled the nice kitins tale and she dint like it so she skratched his eyes out." No wonder Mrs. Jamison had thought I was illiterate!

Wendy knocked on the bathroom door. "Are you all right, Angel? What did Mrs. Jamison say?"

I jammed my fist in my mouth to keep from howling. "Here." I opened the door and handed her the story, glum-faced. "Mrs. Jamison says she's going to fail me. Could I get you to proofread this paper for me?" I asked as she started to read it, eyes glued to the story by virtue of its sheer awfulness. "I think my spelling needs a little work."

"A little?"

My lips twitched, and we both started laughing so hard we had to clutch our sides.

"It was Mike, of course," I said when we'd calmed down. "You've got to help me get back at him for this—and don't you dare tell him I laughed!"

"What did you have in mind?"

"I was reading the personals in the paper this morning. There was an ad from a lady wrestler seeking romance." We walked out of the washroom planning the ad, but Mike scored the next coup in drama class.

Ms. Velez had finally selected the Christmas play—some gothic suspense thing set in a creepy old mansion—and had scheduled tryouts for today.

Much to my parents' pride, I'd played the lead female role in school productions for the past four years. I'd played two wishy-washy simpering heroines, and the part of Laura Morgan, rich girl, in this play looked much the same. I'd decided to try out for the second lead, Laura's spunky friend, Jessie.

Somewhere in the back of my head was the thought that Mike was a shoo-in for the male lead, Giles Foster.

Ms. Velez had her own ideas, however. After watching Maryanne's and Carl's uninspired performances she called Mike and me up on stage.

I balked. "I don't want to try out for Laura; I want to play Jessie."

She didn't seem to hear. "Read Scene One."

Mike smiled down at me. "Come on, Angel. I promise I won't bite."

That did it. I marched up on stage. But I refused to do Scene One, where Laura first arrived at a decrepit mansion and made a fool of herself in front of Giles. I flipped quickly through the script. Didn't Laura have any scenes where she didn't scream or cry or faint?

I finally glimpsed a promising-looking one. "Page fifty-one," I told Mike and launched into furious dialogue: " 'You're just like all the others. All you're interested in is my money!' "

" 'That's not true! Will you listen to me? I can explain.' "

" 'Explain?' " I shriveled him with my contempt. " 'How can you explain? The facts are self-evident.' "

" 'There are extenuating circumstances,' " Mike-Giles pleaded.

" 'Your name isn't Giles Foster, it's Gary McFadden. You lied to me. How can you explain that?' " I demanded passionately, barely glancing at my lines, using Laura's anger to yell at Mike.

" 'Do you hate me?' " He asked the question through white lips, afraid of the answer.

I threw it in his face, just as Laura, hurt and betrayed, would have done. " 'Yes! I hate you, I hate you, I hate you!' " She was hysterical. I skimmed quickly ahead to my next line— *Oh, no!*

I looked up, horrified, and saw Mike swallow a grin before Giles-Gary said grimly, " 'Well, since your opinion of me can't sink any lower, I might as well do this.' "

I looked frantically at Ms. Velez, hoping she'd call a halt to the scene, but it was too late. Mike seized my shoulders and bent me backward in an old-movie-villain-style kiss. A real one, not a stage kiss.

He was just as good at it as I remembered from the pool, damn him.

The other students whistled and clapped until he released me. He bowed to them and then, for my ears only, said, "You needn't have gone to so much trouble just to get kissed. You only had to ask."

My face burned.

Ms. Velez was entranced. "You've got the parts."

"No! I haven't tried out for Jessie yet," I said quickly.

Ms. Velez looked uncertain.

Unexpected support came from Mike. "Oh, let her try Jessie. Angel can play any role she wants."

I tried out for Jessie and had them rolling in the aisles with her country-girl naïveté. Ms. Velez looked thoughtful when I finished. "You'll do."

Maryanne got the part of Laura. "Thanks," she said to me afterward. "I really wanted to play opposite Mike."

But I hadn't done it for her.

Dad was thrilled when I got home and told him about playing Jessie. "Did I ever tell you I used to do some acting back in college?"

"Only about twelve hundred times." I grinned.

"Smart aleck." He grinned back, and it was like old times for a moment.

Mom popped her head in to call us for supper, and the smile leaked away from his face. I remembered the way she used to join in our teasing, and my heart hurt. I didn't understand what was happening.

I thought again about enlisting Mike's help to break up Mom and Mr. Vallant. But we were enemies. . . .

And then it all began to make a terrible kind of sense.

Preoccupied, I washed down my tender T-bone steak with a large glass of milk. I was still thinking furiously, considering angles, when the doorbell rang. I hurried to get it. I had some crazy idea it might be Mr. Vallant, and I wanted to head him off. Instead I opened the door to Coach Hrudey.

"Good evening, Angel. May I come in? I'd like to talk to you and your parents."

Mystified, I led him into the living room.

He introduced himself and shook hands with Dad. "I'm Angel's new gym teacher and badminton coach. As you probably already know, she's exceptionally good."

Mom and Dad managed to disguise their surprise. They knew I liked sports, and they had gone to a lot of my track meets and games over the years, but I'd never mentioned badminton to them in particular. I'd gone to a volleyball camp that summer.

"She and her partner, Mike Vallant"—Mom flinched guiltily—"are the best team I've ever coached, and I don't say that lightly." Coach certainly looked dead serious, but then, I'd never seen him joke around. "Angel is very, very good. I feel that she and Mike have the potential to be Olympic champions."

He startled even me with that announcement. Mom and Dad looked flabbergasted—and uneasy.

"I know, I know." Coach held up a hand as if they had protested. "Badminton is scheduled to be only a demonstration sport at the 1988 Olympics in Seoul, but it will be a medal sport by 1992, when Mike and Angel are in their prime."

Dad's expression clearly said he would never even have thought of that aspect.

Coach kept right on rolling, ruddy face sincere, outlining his qualifications as a coach. He'd competed himself, and he had coached two pairs to Nationals. "With your cooperation, I'd like to start training Angel seriously." He took it totally for granted that I would jump at the chance.

Mom and Dad exchanged glances, the old teamwork still functioning, and Mom spoke for both of them. "I'm afraid you've taken us by surprise, Mr. Hrudey. Angel has always been interested in sports, of course, but the kind of training you're talking about requires a lot of dedication. Angel is in grade eleven, and to be frank, her marks are not that great. I think it would be better for her to concentrate on her studies."

Coach nodded but didn't deviate from his track, like a train bearing down. "You've been very open with me. Now let me be equally honest with you. A year of school can always be made up; an opportunity like this comes along only once in a lifetime. An athlete has only so many years in peak condition, and Angel is already seventeen. She's three years behind the rest of the field already. I believe she has the talent to make up for her late start, but she must start training now."

He made a passionate plea for them not to cost me this opportunity and leave me with a lifetime of regrets.

Mom and Dad were still a bit doubtful but

swayed by his arguments. They looked at each
other.

"Perhaps . . ."

"On a trial basis."

Then together: "What do you think, Angel?"

"Is this something you really want to do?"
Dad asked urgently.

What *did* I think? Olympic gold sounded like
a pipe dream to me, and I was suspicious. What
were the chances of finding two world-class athletes in a small town, population 1,600? And a
coach to boot? It could all be part of some game
plan, but Mom and Dad's nervous uneasiness
made me decide to take a chance.

"Have you talked to Mike yet?" I asked Coach
Hrudey.

"He said yes."

Mike wasn't any keener on partnering me
than I was him. I wondered if he had agreed for
the same reason that I was going to agree.

Escape.

All the traveling involved in competition
would provide opportunities for escape, opportunities that Chinchaga lacked. I'd tried driving
out of Chinchaga once, but had barely gone a
mile when broken glass on the highway made
all four tires go flat. And the glimpse of the next
curve in the river that I'd gotten from the bridge
had shown a series of nets closing off a water
route.

CHAPTER

4

I FOUND MIKE SITTING on my doorstep at six the next morning. Since he was wearing running shoes and shorts it wasn't hard to guess Coach had sent him to be my running partner.

I didn't even pause. I ran right past him.

It was late September, and drifts of soggy yellow leaves clogged the gutters. It had rained the night before, and there was a raw wind, but the exercise kept Mike and me warm.

It also kept us from talking, which was both a blessing and a curse. I didn't feel the sting of Mike's tongue, but the silence was too companionable, too comfortable. I felt compelled to break it.

"First one to the river wins!"

I veered off the smooth sidewalk and into the park, Mike at my heels. We raced breathlessly over hills and obstacles, scrambling across sandpits, jumping over teeter-totters.

The run was wild and reckless. Coach wouldn't have approved. We could have broken an ankle.

Panting, Mike bent forward once we'd stopped. "God, Angel, don't you ever do anything easy?"

"No," I said truthfully.

We ran just as hard on the court, clocking up another mile in short stops and starts in every forty-five–minute match. We played badminton for hours. Drilling, practicing the perfect serve, working on our backhands, learning how to recover from killer smashes and drives, all the while yelling insults at each other: "I've seen cows more graceful than you," "Wimp shot," and "Why don't you just gift-wrap the point for me?"

At first Coach tried to stop our heckling, but he gave up when he realized the competition between us could drive us further than any hope of a medal.

We both bought better rackets, and Coach started us using proper birdies with goose feathers and cork buttons. They flew better, but Mike and I sometimes went through two a session and the little suckers weren't cheap.

We didn't just do drills. We played each other, but more often, because we were supposed to be a team, Coach had us play another mixed doubles pair. "Kyle and Amy are the next best."

I disagreed. "Kyle's good, but if you want someone to wear us into the ground, pick Carl. He has stamina."

"Him?" Coach was incredulous, echoing the same prejudice Wendy's parents had.

"Yes, him." Mike's face turned cold. "Carl happens to be a friend of mine."

Coach backed off, but it wasn't until he saw us play Carl and Wendy that he agreed. Carl had all the power, and Wendy all the strategy. "You're right. Practice with them."

Typically, it didn't seem to occur to him that Carl and Wendy might have something better to do.

"We never get to go out anymore," Wendy complained.

"Sorry." I felt bad. Wendy needed a friend more than anyone I knew—except maybe me. We made plans to go to the movies the next cheap Tuesday to see Arnold Schwarzenegger in *Predator*.

Mike came along. Sometime, when I hadn't been looking, he'd done a despicable thing: he'd become best friends with Carl.

For Wendy and Carl's sake we kept our sniping to a minimum, though Wendy still said, "Shall I check for knife wounds?" twice.

I had to reassure Maryanne three times the next day that Mike and I hadn't been on a date. "He's all yours, really."

"You're probably closer to him than a girl-friend would be anyway," Maryanne said enviously.

It was true. Off the court we still played tricks on each other, but on . . . It frightened me how very good we were together. How we could almost read each other's thoughts, how our motions flowed together like poetry.

And every time we stepped off the court it became harder and harder to stop being a unit, to become cool and distant and safe.

I knew I was in trouble when I started defending Mike to outsiders.

To pinpoint our weaknesses, Coach had made several videotapes of us playing, and he'd finally caught on to our little game. "Look at this!" He replayed several shots. "At first I thought it was just a bad habit on your part, Mike, but then I looked at all the tapes, and you're doing it on purpose—setting Angel up to lose a point!" Coach's face went red, but before he could get too far into his rant I spoke up.

"I asked Mike to set me up for hard shots. I'll never improve if I only get easy ones. If you'll play a little more of the tape, you'll see I do the same for him."

He played the tape, harrumphed, and told us not to do it all the time—it would be a bad habit to fall into during competition. "Zones are only a week away, and I want you to be prepared."

Coach was obsessed with Zones, which would be our first tournament and would decide which badminton teams in our region went on to Provincials. He'd drilled into us that we had to win.

I was confident that Mike and I could win—if we were allowed to leave Chinchaga, at all.

The first attempt to stop us happened on Monday. I showed up for practice and found Mike smashing birdies against the wall.

"Temper, temper," I said.

Mike didn't respond to my taunt. "They're not going to let me go to the badminton tournament." His voice was stark.

The words turned a key inside me. *Escape.* "Why not?"

"My parents say"—*smash*—"that tournaments are expensive"—*smash*—"and they can't afford it." *Smash.* Mike looked up, sweat running down his face. "Looks as though you're short a partner."

"Not a chance," I said, and went to find Coach. It didn't take much to fire him up, and within fifteen minutes the three of us were at Mike's house, talking to Mrs. Vallant.

Coach gave his "lifetime of regrets" spiel again, harping on the Olympics. He pointed out that Mike's absence would punish the entire badminton team and offered to pay for Mike's hotel room and meals out of his own pocket.

Mrs. Vallant was unprepared for the offer and stalled. "We really couldn't impose on you like that."

"It isn't an imposition. I donate money to sports scholarships every year because I believe that athletes with drive and talent deserve a chance to compete," Coach said earnestly.

She had more objections, but Coach shot them all down, and she finally relented, more to make Coach go away than because she felt bad about standing in the way of her son's success.

The incident pleased me in an odd way because it proved that the badminton tournament wasn't part of the game plan; that Coach had come up with it on his own.

Afterward, Mike and I stood on the sidewalk and grinned at each other.

"Getting Coach to talk to her was brilliant." Mike slung his arm around my shoulders. "I don't know about you, but I feel like sinking my teeth into a juicy hamburger and to hell with Coach's dry chicken diet. You want to come along?"

The invitation was casual, a buddy thing, not a date, but it still froze me because I was so very close to saying yes. "No. I've got to get home."

My offhand tone didn't fool Mike. He dropped his arm, his gaze intense. "What do you have against me, anyway? Can't you see what a good team we'd make? What a good team we *do* make?"

I lashed out at him. "Of course I do! That's the whole point, dummy. We make too good a team. *We're too much alike.*"

He hadn't known.

Realization dilated his pupils, and he took a step back. Violet eyes met violet eyes for an electric second, before I fled as if pursued by a pack of werewolves.

CHAPTER

5

I DODGED MIKE the next morning by going for my run an hour earlier, but there was no avoiding him at school. He brushed by me in the hall, eyes searing my face like lasers, and slipped a piece of paper into my jacket pocket.

The note burned a hole in my coat lining all through math class. I didn't want to open it. It couldn't help; it could only tempt me.

I finally gave in during social studies, while Wendy's father was lecturing us on the Renaissance. I opened the note inside my desk, careful to appear as if I was merely fumbling with my pencil case.

"We have to talk."

I tore it in half, put it in my mouth, and chewed it into spitballs. I had to shoot two at Wendy to get her attention. She looked irritated, then amused.

I passed a note across the row to her as if we

were third graders. "I declare today Shock the Teacher Day."

Wendy looked at it, then passed it to Maryanne, who was sitting in front of her.

Maryanne read it, glanced at me, then passed it on.

I was watching it change hands a seventh time when Mr. Lindstrom said my name. He knew something was going on, but not what. "Why don't you start, Angel?"

I didn't have the faintest idea what he was talking about.

"Go on." He smiled faintly, gray eyes crinkling behind his glasses. "Read your paper to the class."

In a flash I remembered the one-page paper on the Renaissance he'd assigned last class. I hadn't done it, of course. He'd made the mistake of telling us at the beginning of the semester exactly how much percent of our final mark each assignment was worth. It was my practice not to do assignments unless they were worth at least five percent.

Mr. Lindstrom never failed to admonish me for it when I was visiting Wendy. It was our running joke. He fully expected to catch me flat-footed this time, too.

Instead I stood up and gave a short speech on the Renaissance man. In fifteenth-century Italy a man was not thought accomplished if he was good at only one thing, like swordplay. A gentleman was expected to be good at swordsmanship *and* poetry *and* statecraft. Leonardo da Vinci was not just a painter, but an architect and an inventor, too.

Mr. Lindstrom looked surprised and pleased when I finished. At last he'd caught my interest! I wondered what he would have thought if he'd known that I'd gleaned most of my information from reading historical romance novels.

"May I see your paper?"

That was the crowning touch. I opened up my binder and handed him a sheet of blank paper.

The class howled.

Other teachers were destined to be shocked that day as well. The whole English 20 class stood up and sang out, "Good morning, Mrs. Jamison," when she walked in, and the students behaved with perfect manners all period, paying strict attention and putting up their hands before speaking. Everyone in Ms. Velez's drama class affected a Russian accent. Wendy kissed crusty old Mr. Heron on the cheek, and Mike "accidentally" dropped a flake of sodium into some water in chemistry class. The flake immediately underwent oxidation—it burned.

I didn't see all of the pranks, but I heard Mr. Lindstrom laughing about it with Raven that night when I was downstairs with Wendy. For the first time in a month I skipped badminton practice. I told Mom that Wendy had invited me over, even though I'd invited myself. I partly wanted to avoid the tension at home and partly wanted to avoid Mike.

"So what's up?" Wendy asked me. "I thought

you were dead serious about this Olympic stuff."

"I am." I shrugged restlessly. "I just wanted an evening off from Mike. You know how he gets on my nerves."

Wendy was silent for a long beat. "I thought you two were getting along better lately."

I stared at her incredulously. "You saw us at the theater. We couldn't even agree on what kind of popcorn to get."

She didn't look convinced, so I launched into a long list of Mike's faults.

"You know," Wendy said thoughtfully, "if I didn't know better I'd swear you liked Mike." My laugh must have rung a little hollow, because she paused. "You don't, do you?" She was thinking about Maryanne. Maryanne liked Mike, and friends didn't poach on other friends' crushes.

"Of course not." I met her gaze square on, and she seemed satisfied. It was a useful trick I'd learned at age four when I was still in the Orphanage.

"I don't understand why you're so set against him. You liked him until he introduced himself on the bridge, don't tell me you didn't."

I didn't want to answer. "I'll tell you, if you tell me why you hate your dad."

Wendy slouched deeper into the couch. "I don't hate him," she mumbled. "I'm just very, very angry with him."

I raised an eyebrow. "For eight months?"

"Longer than that." Her breath came in on a harsh laugh. "Try four years."

Raven had said Wendy came to live with them four years ago.

"What did he do to make you so mad?" I asked.

"Nothing." Her gaze became dark and brooding. "That's what I blame him for. He did nothing, and I didn't tell him, and Lee died. If I forgive him, then I have to blame myself." She clenched her fists, her friendship bracelets brushing her scarred knuckles.

"Who's Lee?"

"My brother." Wendy got up abruptly, 115 pounds of leashed energy. It was clear she didn't want to talk about it any more. "Your turn. What's the story with you and Mike?"

There could have been a hundred listening devices in the room, but Wendy had bared herself to me. I gave her a portion of the truth: "We're competitors. I feel as though he's stealing my friends, my place in our group. I'm not the Idea Girl anymore."

My turn to change the subject. "What are you going to get Maryanne for her birthday?" I asked.

"I don't know, probably earrings. I'm broke." Wendy had lied to get money from her dad, saying she needed it to go to the movies. Then she'd turned around and spent that and her last month's allowance on a beautiful fish mobile for her brother-to-be.

"Earrings are boring. Besides, she's got lots of earrings. We need to think of something interesting and unusual." I tipped my head back, putting my brain into idea mode. "Something her parents haven't already bought her." Maryanne had a car of her own, skis, a stereo, a Commodore 64 computer, and enough clothes for twins.

"Something cheap," Wendy added.

"Interesting, unusual, and cheap," I repeated. "Plus, it should be something she wants."

Wendy snorted. "Maryanne wants Mike. Why don't we gift-wrap him?"

The idea appealed to me. "That's perfect! Let's get her a boyfriend. Not Mike, though. He'll break her heart into little bitty pieces." I remembered all the hearts with Mike's initials scrawled on the bathroom walls in all those schools.

"You're serious?" Wendy read the answer on my face, and her lips twitched. "Well, it's certainly inexpensive. But who else, if not Mike?"

I remembered Jimmy's yearning eyes. "Jimmy. You know he likes her."

"Jimmy's also as shy as a fence post. No way could you get him to dress up in a box."

I raised an eyebrow. "Want to bet?"

I began the campaign the next day. I waited until school let out, then got Jimmy's attention in the time-honored way: I dropped a pile of books on his toes.

While he hopped around on one foot, I apologized and started hastily gathering up the books, but by design I had far too many and kept dropping them. Jimmy ended up carrying them out to the parking lot for me.

I scanned the parking lot. "My ride's not here yet. Do you have to go anywhere?"

Jimmy shook his head. He really was tongue-tied.

"I have to go shopping for Maryanne's present. Are you coming to the party?"

"Yes."

I chattered on, about how I wasn't sure what to get her, and how boys had it easier than girls did picking out presents. Had he already bought Maryanne a present?

Another nod. Jimmy believed in the pulling-teeth method of conversation.

"What did you get her?"

"Jumper cables. She always forgets to turn off the lights on her car."

It was a thoughtful, practical gift—and Maryanne would hate it. "Look, you can tell me to go jump off a bridge if you want, but do you like Maryanne?"

He nodded.

"I mean *like* like her, as a girl and not just as a friend?"

His Adam's apple bobbed, and his face turned as red as his hair, making his freckles stand out. "Yes."

"Then take my advice and give her flowers. A single red rose. Roses are romantic," I said firmly. "Jumper cables aren't."

He smiled faintly. "Got it."

"And you can't just give the rose to her," I said, warming to my theme. "You have to make her notice it. Make a gesture of it." I started to get excited as I planned aloud. The gift-wrapped box was the least flamboyant idea I suggested, but Jimmy wouldn't go for any of them. For someone quiet he was surprisingly stubborn. I found myself liking him for it.

"Okay, no grand gestures, but make sure you arrive after everyone else so you aren't lost in a rush of other people's gifts, and kiss her on the cheek, okay?"

Jimmy thought he could handle that.

I pretended I'd spotted my ride, grabbed the rest of the books, and backed away. "And a card. Make sure you give her a birthday card, a sweet romantic one, not a joke, okay?"

"Okay."

I hurried toward a strange car until I heard Jimmy drive off, then dumped my books back inside the school—I'd claim them from Lost and Found in the morning—and started walking home.

Mike pulled up alongside me halfway home, window down and music blasting. I expected him to ask for a chance to talk again, but he must have known I would refuse. "I saw you talking to Jimmy. What was that all about?"

I smiled a secret smile. "Nothing."

"You're up to something," Mike said flatly. "And I'm going to find out what." He drove off.

When I got home I found Mom crying on the sofa. Her eyes were red, and about half a box of used tissues lay in a pile on the floor.

When I asked her what was wrong, all she would say was that she and Dad had had a fight. She avoided my eyes. "I'm not sure if he's coming home for supper. Or ever." She said the last words very softly as she got up and went into the kitchen, but I heard them and felt like breaking things.

Dad did come home, at about seven-thirty, and ate cold leftovers alone in the kitchen.

At nine o'clock Mom knocked on my bedroom door and asked me to come down to the living room. "There's something we want to talk to you about."

My heart banged like a drum. *This is it. They're going to tell me they're getting a divorce.* Tension, anger, and fear formed a lead ball in my stomach as I followed Mom down the stairs. I slumped in the armchair, and Mom and Dad perched on opposite ends of the couch.

Dad spoke first and what he said was such a relief that I almost laughed aloud. "Your mother and I are concerned about your marks. We allowed you to train with Coach Hrudey on the condition that you would not neglect your schoolwork. I'm afraid we can't allow you to compete in the badminton tournament this weekend because you're failing some of your classes."

I quelled a grin and struggled to concentrate. No way was I going to miss the badminton tournament. "Which classes am I failing?"

"Social studies," Dad said.

"And math," Mom said.

I shook my head. "I have a sixty-two percent in math, and I'm getting an A in drama and phys ed. My only other class is a study block."

"One class is still too many," Dad said.

"I have a social studies test on Wednesday. If I

can pull up my mark to a B, can I play in the tournament?"

"Mr. Lindstrom tells us you have forty-five percent at the moment, dear. It's impossible."

"If I do it, can I go?" I repeated.

"Yes, but—"

I kissed Dad's cheek. "Guess I better go hit the books, huh?"

I went upstairs, still buoyant with relief, and did some quick math. I had 45 percent right now out of the 30 percent that made up our final social studies mark. The next test was worth 20 percent of our final mark, so I needed to get a 95 percent or better to bring my mark up to a 65 percent.

No problem.

One A in a long list of C's wouldn't give me away.

Still, I made a big deal about studying for four hours that night and four more hours the next. I got Wendy to quiz me at noon hour. By the time the social studies test actually rolled around, I knew the material so well I could have written a book on the subject.

I sat well across the room from Wendy and kept my eyes glued to my test until I handed it in. I couldn't risk any accusations of cheating.

I had requested ahead of time that Mr. Lindstrom mark my test by the next day so I could go to the badminton tournament if I passed. He had said yes quite kindly, but I knew from his face on Thursday that he didn't really believe I could do it.

"Ninety-eight percent. Congratulations, Angel."

"Yes!" I leaped out of my seat to get my test paper back.

"I'm amazed," Mr. Lindstrom said. He didn't accuse me of cheating, although he must have been under pressure to do so. "I was sure you weren't paying attention when we covered Niccolò Machiavelli's book, *The King*, last week."

"*The Prince*, you mean." I grinned. Another bullet dodged.

Mike and I would leave for the tournament tomorrow.

In the meantime, there was Maryanne's birthday party to attend that night.

I'd been there for close to an hour when Maryanne went to answer the doorbell and found a large gift-wrapped box sitting outside.

I was surprised and delighted that Jimmy had changed his mind after all, until Maryanne blushingly pulled open the box and revealed Mike standing there instead.

CHAPTER

6

MIKE TOOK THE ROSE from between his teeth and presented it to Maryanne with a small bow. "For you, milady. Happy birthday.

He'd stolen my idea! I gritted my teeth with outrage. I would have shared my anger with Wendy, but she had come down with one of her frequent bouts of flu and had stayed home.

Maryanne took it the wrong way, of course. She saw it as a romantic gesture aimed at her rather than a monkey wrench in my plans. She smiled up at Mike, and, after shooting a smirk in my direction, he smiled back down at her.

Jimmy slunk in half an hour later, mumbling something about the rose dying. I wondered if Mike had told him to put it in hot water. Jimmy gave Maryanne a present shaped suspiciously like jumper cables, but she didn't even unwrap it, just laid it on a table with some other gifts.

We went downstairs to Maryanne's basement. Her parents were two floors up and tolerant of loud music. Their basement was furnished as nicely as most living rooms, and there was a small dance floor in the center.

When "Take My Breath Away" by Berlin came on, Mike and Maryanne started dancing. Maryanne floated like a delicate brown-haired pixie in his arms, and it made me furious. I didn't let myself think about why I was so angry, just turned to Jimmy with a diamond-hard smile. "The game's not over yet. Let's dance."

As I had expected, knowing Mike's coordination on the court, he was a good dancer. Maryanne was pretty good herself, and their steps were light and intricate.

Dancing with Jimmy was like walking to music. Even Carl had more rhythm.

Dancing so close—there were three other couples on the small floor—it was easy to position ourselves near Mike and Maryanne. As the song wound down I whispered to Jimmy, "Change partners."

He looked a little doubtful but cleared his throat and asked Maryanne. She said yes politely, but her eyes lingered on Mike.

Before I could step off to the side, Mike took my arm. "Not so fast. Dance with me."

I started dancing to keep him occupied, but my motives soon stopped being so pure. REO Speedwagon sang "Can't Fight This Feeling," and the music lifted me, transported me. Mike and I moved together, point and counterpoint, striking the same bittersweet chord of rightness that our play on the court did.

Mike felt it, too. His face became blank, guarded—like mine. I had a public face and a hidden private one, my heart like a clenched fist.

Maryanne would bruise herself on him and not even know why.

Wendy had repeated a riddle to me once that Mike had made up. Question: "What's an angel's smile?" Answer: "The amount of energy required to light a hundred candles."

I smiled at him. Incandescently.

He stumbled for a second, off-balance. "What are you up to now, Angel?"

"Nothing." I kept smiling into his eyes, the music thrumming in my ears, keeping time with my blood, and we danced, our movements perfectly in tune—

Jimmy jarred his elbow, and Mike tore his gaze away. He was breathing too fast, but his voice was even. "Nice try." When the song faded away, he asked Maryanne to dance again.

Janet Jackson's "Nasty" flooded the speakers. Jimmy sat out, defeated, so I asked Sean to dance. (He'd forgiven me once word got out that Coach Hrudey was training me for the Olympics.) "Let's show them how it's done," I said. Sean was a flashy dancer, and we did a few moves we'd patented back when we were dating.

Mike and Maryanne immediately copied the moves and added a little fillip of their own.

I copied it right back and added something

extra. Sean kept up easily. We soon had a contest going, with the other couples cheering.

Maryanne finally dropped out, pleading exhaustion, and Mike sat out with her. Sean and I pulled out all the stops for the next song, but it wasn't the same.

The hopeful look on Sean's face pricked at my conscience, so when Maryanne's mother brought down cake, I quietly detached myself from Sean and drifted back over to where Jimmy was standing. "We'll watch movies next. Try to sit by Maryanne."

Jimmy nodded dispiritedly, not up to arguing.

I tried to insert myself between Mike and Maryanne on the couch, but Mike outmaneuvered me. I ended up wedged between the couch arm and him.

In addition to the cake, Maryanne's mother had set out bowls of chips and candy all over the room. I pointed to the bowl of M&M's on the coffee table. "Can you pass me some?"

Maryanne passed them along, taking a handful herself. She fed one to Mike. "M&M's. Mike and Maryanne, get it?"

Mike gritted his teeth and smiled. One point for me.

But I didn't feel the usual rush of elation. What did our little war matter? Before the end of the night Mike and Maryanne would be dating.

I turned blindly toward the VCR and watched ten minutes of *Beverly Hills Cop* in silence.

When the vertical hold went haywire, freezing the picture, I was relieved. I was seriously considering going home early when Mike suggested playing hide-and-seek in the dark.

My eyebrows went up—we were a little old for hide-and-seek—but everyone made enthusiastic noises, and Mike set out the rules: No turning on the lights or going outside. If you made it back to the white couch before the person who was It found you, you were safe. The people who were caught couldn't hide again or help It.

We pulled all the blinds to shut out the streetlights, left Maryanne counting to one hundred with her eyes closed, and spread out in the dark.

Quite a few people went upstairs or hid in the closets. I was more familiar with Maryanne's house than most; I slipped into the laundry room.

There was a small door there leading to a space under the stairs. Maryanne would find me eventually, but she didn't like the dark. She would search upstairs first and find someone else to be It.

I was just opening the door when somebody slipped inside the room. My eyes weren't fully adjusted to the meager light coming through the half-buried basement window, but even in the dark I knew it was Mike.

That's how far gone I was. I recognized him in the dark.

I opened my mouth to tell him to leave, but Mike lifted a finger to his lips, a gray outline. Footsteps passed by in the hall: Maryanne.

I waited until she had gone up the stairs. "Get lost in the dark?" I asked sarcastically.

A faint smile curled the corners of his mouth. "Yes."

Liar. There was no point in asking him to leave so I started toward the door. Mike blocked me.

I stared at him in furious disbelief and a little fear. He was my equal in strength. I couldn't move him if I tried and certainly not without making noise. It dawned on me that this had been his aim all along, not Maryanne. His note: "We have to talk."

I turned my back to him. He could keep me here, but he couldn't make me look at him.

"Angel—"

"And another thing"—I rounded on him in whispered fury as if we were in the middle of an argument—"don't say my name like that!"

"Like what—Angel?" The word became an endearment on his tongue.

"You know!"

Unexpectedly, Mike relented. "Yeah, I guess I do." He moved away from the door, toward me. There was nowhere to retreat in the small room, and I didn't try. My vision was improving by the second, and I could see his face. It was as serious as his voice. "It's not going to work, is it?"

I blinked rapidly. "What isn't going to work?"

He didn't answer, only coming closer so that we stood face-to-face.

Us. He meant us. The blood drained from my face, my control crumbling with it. "Why can't you just leave me alone?" Everything had been so simple before he came along.

Mike considered my words as if the idea had occurred to him for the first time. "Leave you alone? I don't think I can." Then he was kissing me wildly, and I was kissing him back.

We didn't break apart until Maryanne cried, "You're It!" somewhere upstairs.

My breathing was choppy, and I felt like weeping. "We have to stop."

Mike nibbled on my neck. "Why?"

"Because they'll see."

"Nobody can see in the dark," Mike said logically.

I thought of infrared goggles and listening devices. But we were in a laundry room. . . .

He started kissing me again, and I twisted my head aside. "Don't you get it? We're playing right into their hands. This is what they've wanted from the very beginning."

"I prefer to think of it as joining forces." I felt the touch of his fingers on my back like a brand.

"*No*. They want to study us because we're different, unique."

Mike already knew that. "So?"

"So how do you get more unique people, Mike?" Tears gathered in the back of my throat. "You breed them together. You get them to make *babies*."

His arms fell to his sides.

I pressed on. "Do you know what their next step is? Can't you guess? Tell me, Mike, have your parents been having fights lately?"

His face hardened. "They always fight. It's nothing new."

"Well, it's new for my parents," I said bitterly. "You've seen them together, haven't you? Your dad and my mom, sneaking around, letting us see them. They're going to get divorced and marry each other. You and I will end up living in the same house with rooms across the hall from each other. Won't that be convenient?"

Mike didn't get a chance to answer because Maryanne came back down the stairs, talking to the other kids. "I think we're still missing Angel and Mike."

She couldn't find us together. I couldn't betray her like that. Quick as a flash I ducked out the laundry room, ran down the hall and made a dive for the couch. "Safe!"

Laughing, the rest of the party trooped back down the stairs. Maryanne triumphantly produced Mike within a matter of minutes.

"Well, I'm going home now," I told Maryanne, head down, one foot already on the stairs.

Before I could claim to have a headache, Mike spoke up. "Me, too. Coach will kill us if we don't get a full eight hours' sleep before the tournament." He hustled me up the stairs ahead of him. "I'll give you a ride home."

What Maryanne thought about her date leaving with me I couldn't bear to look and see.

The second we were outside, I jerked away from Mike. "You snake! What about Maryanne?"

He laughed, he actually laughed, and I came very close to decking him. "Maryanne was in on it," he said. "I told her I liked you, and we planned the whole thing between us."

Planned. The. Whole. Thing.

I remembered how Jimmy hadn't been able to look me in the eye. "Jimmy, too?"

He nodded.

I kicked him in the shin and started walking.

"Ouch!" Mike followed me for a few steps, then turned back. I heard the sound of a car engine turning over, and he backed out of the driveway. I kept walking.

He drove past me.

A block later he parked his car and fell into step beside me. I could have yelled at him again, but I didn't. I stopped fighting the tide once and for all, and we walked to the park in oddly peaceful silence. I removed my running shoes and went down to the river.

Mike did the same. We didn't speak until we were at the bottom of the riverbank, far from any picnic tables, listening to the liquid syllables of the river's flow. "You really think this is necessary?" he said.

"Yes." I had personally washed all the clothes I was wearing, but there could be listening or tracking devices in the soles of our shoes. I rolled up my jeans and waded into the water to give an excuse for having bare feet.

Mike came in after me and cupped my face in his hands. He studied me for a moment, violet eyes intense. "God, Angel, do I terrify you half as much as you terrify me?"

"More," I said, and our lips met again.

Mike finally pulled back and rested his forehead against mine. "You've been driving me crazy since I introduced myself on the bridge and you decided I had two heads. How did you know so soon? Was it the eyes? I'd forgotten we all had the same color eyes."

"No. I knew about you from the trophies." I explained about all the towns we'd both lived in. "I think the reason they move us so often is so we won't notice that the whole population of the town changes over a two-year period. Even though your name was always on the trophy for the previous year, only about half of my class-mates and teachers would remember you—and half of those would move away during the year I lived in that town."

Mike nodded. "The towns are like movie sets. The casts change except for our parents."

I wondered exactly how Mike had come by his awful mother and father. I'd had a choice of about eight pairs when I selected mine. Except for the lies standing between us, for all intents and pur-poses they *were* my parents; Mike's were just actors playing the part of his mother and father.

"Our parents and Uncle Albert and Aunt Patty," I agreed. The pair of so-called relatives had come for periodic visits to all the towns I had lived in—obviously spies sent to evaluate me for the scientists.

"Mine were Uncle Arthur and Aunt Phyllis," Mike said.

"I bet they're the same people. I once took a photo of Uncle Albert, but—wouldn't you know it?—the film was 'accidentally' exposed to light and ruined."

Mike wasn't listening. "How much do you remember?" he asked me. "About the Orphanage?"

"More than I should, considering how young I was at the time." I was only three or four years old when I left. "I remember the tests: 'What's five to the ninth power? If you tell me you can have ice cream for dessert.'"

Mike nodded. "Two or three tests every day. Lots of math."

"And the doctors." They had played at being teachers, but I knew them now for scientists. They had never been truly comfortable with so many children, always slightly stiff, their smiles false.

"I remember that they never let us just play," Mike said, hands shoved in his pockets. "It always had to be a contest. They encouraged us to compete with one another."

"We hardly ever went outside. And when we did, it was just to the enclosed playground in the center of the building." Leaving the Orphanage had been like being let out of prison. I still took pleasure in the simple feel of sun shining on my face.

Mike looked out across the water. "The better you did on the tests, the more tests you had to take."

"So we all played dumb." *Nikita had pulled me aside one day at lunchtime. "They're watching you," he had told me. "If you don't want to be locked up inside all day, don't answer so many of their questions."*

"I remember the fire," Mike said softly.

Ferocious heat. Screaming. A flaming roof and timbers collapsing. "They kept the doors locked at all times to prevent us from escaping," I said. "The sprinklers were supposed to put out any fires that started, but they didn't work." Sabotage.

The scientists had tried to keep the knowledge from me, but I knew a lot of children had died in the fire, somewhere in the range of thirty to forty. And more than a few had escaped as well.

"And then there was no more Orphanage." Mike changed the subject. "So what now? I presume you've been doing the same as me, playing dumb, killing time until you're old enough to make a living once you break out of the movie set."

"Pretty much." I hesitated. "I'm going to try a breakout once we start competing in badminton. I think Coach is for real, and he took the scientists by surprise. They didn't have time to plan a strategy."

"Funny," Mike said, "I had almost exactly the same idea. Would you mind some company?"

"I'd love some," I said softly. "To escape." We made a pact together on our clenched fists, while the water flowed cold around our ankles.

"We'd better head back," Mike said abruptly, "before they send out a search party."

I nodded reluctantly. He was right, but I didn't want to go just yet, to give this up.

I'd been fighting alone for so long.

"Angel?"

"I'm coming." I waded out of the river.

"You realize, of course," he said lightly, "that we'll have to pretend to be dating, so we don't arouse their suspicion."

My heart turned to stone inside my breast, and I stopped dead.

Mike noticed. I couldn't hide myself from him the way I could from others. "What is it? What are you thinking?"

"The same thing you are." My heart pounded. "That if you're lying to me, if you're on the scientists' side, I'll carve your heart out with a dull knife."

Mike laughed at my fierceness, the sound wild and bitter. "Close." He kissed me twice on the lips, sipping from them greedily. "I was thinking that the scientists would be stupid to trust us if one of us *is* in their pay, because we'd be sure to double-cross them."

CHAPTER

7

I MADE SURE MY PARENTS saw Mike kiss me good night at the door before going in.

My parents were shocked.

"Was that Mike?" Dad asked.

I nodded.

"But I thought you hated him," Mom said. She and Dad both looked bewildered—and a little relieved.

"I did." I didn't explain my change of heart, and they were too cautious to ask.

I wanted to ask Mom if, now that Mike and I were dating, the farce with Mr. Vallant would stop. I had to bite my lip to keep the question back.

I had difficulty falling asleep that night. My mind kept racing on a treadmill: thinking about Mike, thinking about the badminton tournament, thinking about my parents, thinking about Mike and me at the tournament.

The scientists had already made two attempts to keep Mike and me from attending Zones, but the competition was scheduled for Thursday night. The bus would leave after school tomorrow. What else could they do?

I underestimated them.

When I got up in the middle of the night to go downstairs to get a glass of milk, I tripped over a heavy box at the top of the stairs.

My eyes were still half closed, and I hadn't turned on the light. The box hit my left leg at shin level, and I fell.

If I'd grabbed the rail, I would have wrenched my arm, and I needed my arm to play badminton. The nature of the stairs, dropping away in the dark, aided me and gave me time to get my hands under me and kick up my legs. I pushed off the fourth step with my hands, cartwheeled down the stairs, and landed hard at the bottom, but on my feet, not my arms. I didn't even twist my ankle.

The thumps woke my parents. The lights came on, and they both appeared at the top of the stairs.

"Angel? What is it? Are you all right?" Dad asked.

I sank down against the living room wall and started to cry.

Mom hurried toward me and almost tripped on the box herself. "What's this doing here? Did you fall? Oh, my God, Angel!"

They weren't in on it. They hadn't known. I cried harder in my relief.

Mom helped me up, depositing me on the living room sofa. She turned on more lights and checked me over carefully. Had I hurt myself? Was I okay? Should she call a doctor? She didn't wait for my reply. "I'm going to call a doctor." She stood up.

"No." My voice was hoarse, but it stopped her. "The tournament's tomorrow."

Dad caught on first. Black rage filled his face. He caught my mother's arm when she would have gone to the phone. "No, Eileen. Angel's okay. She doesn't want to go to the doctor, do you?"

I shook my head. Adrenaline crashed through my system. The stairs were carpeted and only one flight long. I probably wouldn't have been killed by the fall, but a sprained wrist, a concussion, and a broken leg were all distinct possibilities.

Dad carried the box down from the top of the stairs. It contained Mom's old sewing machine, which we kept in the basement. While I watched, he very methodically smashed the whole thing to pieces.

I insisted on doing some stretches to prevent stiffness before I went back to bed. Mom sat by my bedside. I fell asleep only to wake up again and hear Dad yelling at someone on the phone. Mom was still there. She stroked my hair, and her hand trembled. "Go back to sleep."

I needed to be rested for the tournament so I closed my eyes and slept again.

Coach had instructed Mike and me not to go

for a run that morning, so I didn't see Mike until I got to school. I examined him anxiously from across the hall. No cast, no limp, no black stitches crawling caterpillar-wise across his forehead.

"Hey there," Mike said, smiling at me.

I wasn't alone anymore. I had a partner. "Hey yourself." I walked across the hall, hooked an arm around his neck and kissed him lingeringly.

Wendy was gaping when we finished, but as soon as she found out that Maryanne didn't mind and even seemed to be interested in Jimmy, she was happy. "I knew it!" she kept saying. "Now we can double-date."

Carl shook his head. "Talk about an unholy alliance. You and Angel are bad enough together," he told Wendy. "Add Mike to the mix and . . . there might not be a building in town left standing after you three get through with it."

The bell rang and I was forced to wait until noon hour before I could tell Mike what had happened the night before. We sat close together on the grass outside under the guise of cuddling.

"I had a little mishap last night." In retelling it, I made it sound almost like fun. "Fastest way to go downstairs," I joked.

Mike didn't laugh. He swore under his breath and hugged me.

I felt instantly better, which was scary. How could Mike come to mean so much to me in such a short time? Yesterday I had still been convinced that I hated him.

"There's something I want to talk to you about," Mike whispered while nibbling on my neck.

"What?" I breathed, but although he continued to drop kisses on my face, his next words weren't romantic at all.

"After Coach's big recruiting speech, I looked up badminton in the almanac. Do you know what it said? It said badminton would become a medal sport in 1992, but mixed doubles aren't scheduled to be added until 1996."

I ran my fingers through Mike's hair. "So you think it is a scientists' trick after all, and Coach is a much better actor than we thought?"

Mike shook his head. "I think he's training us for the Olympics, all right, just not the 1992 games."

I looked at him quizzically.

"Two years ago there was a boy in my class who didn't know how to use a rotary-dial telephone."

The implications rocked through me. "Wendy sometimes makes small slips," I said. I told him about the fines she had mentioned and her strange question as to whether I had known Mike "Before, or should I say After."

I kissed his chin, murmuring, "And come to think of it, when Maryanne first moved to Chinchaga she called good-looking boys 'chunks' instead of 'hunks.'"

Mike traced my jawline with his finger. "People who just recently moved to town always rave about the low prices."

"Hell," I said, careful to whisper, careful to keep my head turned in such a way that my lips couldn't be read, "We're not living in a movie set; we're living in a museum."

"That was my hypothesis, too." Mike pretended to smell my hair.

It would have to be a very realistic museum, a reenactment of history, with all the players but us in on it and trained to use the right slang and act like people living in 1987.

I fed Mike a section of orange from my lunch. "We need proof."

If Mike and I were right, in addition to fines for talking about anything from the future, there must also be a stricture against bringing in anything technologically advanced or with a clear date on it.

But of course some people had probably cheated.

I remembered Wendy cramming some kind of candy bar in her mouth when I visited her unexpectedly, eating the evidence and stuffing the wrapper in her jeans pocket.

Maryanne's parents were gadget lovers and sure to have brought something with them. Wendy's dad might have a couple of books with a later copyright date stuffed in among his five-hundred-some collection. But, after some discussion, Mike and I decided Coach was our best bet.

"Remember how upset he was when you beat him at singles and told him we couldn't be all that good if we had so much trouble beating someone his age?" Mike asked.

My lips twitched. I had said, "No offense, Coach," but of course he had taken offense. "I'm a former O"—he'd stopped and corrected himself—"a former champion, not some old man off the street! Not many people alive can beat me."

"He started to say 'Olympic champion,' I'm sure of it," Mike said.

"Which means that somewhere he has an Olympic medal," I finished for Mike. "Coach couldn't bear to leave that behind. And medals have dates on them."

So during the fifteen minutes between school being let out for the day and the time when our bus was to leave, Mike dragged Coach Hrudey off with him to check the bus tires, which he swore were too low, while I zipped into Coach's office for a little burglary.

Coach could have hidden his medal at home of course, but the last time I'd been in his office to watch videotapes of Mike and me playing badminton something in his display case had struck me as odd.

The case wasn't locked, and I slid back the glass door easily. Inside were two badminton rackets and a birdie, a couple of badminton trophies, undated, and a football.

It might have seemed normal to any of the censors that a phys ed teacher would own a football, but I'd never heard Coach mention any sport except badminton. He lived and breathed it. He never knew when the Edmonton Eskimos won or lost, and he never talked about baseball or basketball.

I picked up the football and quickly ran my fingers over the lacings. I tugged open the small zipper I found and reached inside. My fingers scissored closed around a small packet. Through the paper I could feel something circular.

My heart was beating painfully fast and I was convinced that Coach, or somebody else, would come by any second and catch me in the act, so I shoved the package in my pocket without opening it up. I quickly zipped the football back up, replaced it in the display case, closed the glass door, and went out to the bus.

One of the tires was low and was being pumped up while Coach stood over the driver, fuming. Attempt number four to keep us in Chinchaga had been foiled.

Mike looked a question at me, and I nodded, but I didn't dare take out the package with so many people around.

Twenty minutes later we were on board and the bus was under way. Mike and I sat together in the backseat. In addition to Mike, me, and Coach Hrudey, there was another mixed doubles team, Kyle and Amy, two men's singles players, and one women's singles entrant.

Spirits were high, and Mike and I had to wait through "Ninety-nine Bottles of Beer" before things finally got quiet enough, and dim enough, to examine the package.

As quietly as possible, I unwrapped the paper in my pocket, then pulled the medal out, being careful not to let any of the striped ribbon show. I held it cupped in my two hands letting in just enough light so we could read it. It was gold, as I had expected. "Men's Singles, Badminton," it said, "2089."

"A hundred years from now," I whispered. Even though I had suspected, it was terrible to have it confirmed. A shaft of ice went up my spine.

Mike was shaking his head. "More than a hundred," he whispered back. "Coach was probably in his twenties when he won, and he must be close to forty now."

One hundred ten to one hundred twenty years in the future. My hand began to shake. I almost dropped the medal. Mike pocketed it quickly and pressed my head against his shoulder. "I know," he said. "I know."

One hundred twenty years ago, in 1867, Canada had just become a country. The United States had recently fought a civil war with cavalry and cannons instead of atomic bombs and napalm. I'd been on a school trip once to Fort Edmonton with its log cabins and railroad and blacksmith shop. The other kids had rolled their eyes and laughed. "Not *another* one," they'd said. Another museum, they'd meant.

The world I'd grown up in was as obsolete as that blacksmith shop.

What had the scientists done to us?

I stopped feeling bad about borrowing Coach's medal. He had lied to me. Everyone I had ever met had lied to me on a fundamental level.

I wanted to scream and shout and accuse.

I didn't speak for close to an hour, bottling up the rage. I stared out the window at the forests and fields and thought about my enemies, the scientists who had done this to Mike and me. They had done very personal damage to my life, but if I passed them on the street I wouldn't know who they were, except for Uncle Albert and Aunt Patty. I hated Uncle Albert and Aunt Patty more because they were the only faces I had to attach to my enemies than because of anything they did, although they had done enough.

Fat Uncle Albert with his Trojan Horse gifts: telescopes, chemistry sets, chessboards. I remembered him roping me into a game of chess with him at Christmastime when I was ten. "Chess is the game of kings," he'd told me. "A game of strategy. Come on, play with me. *I'll let you win.*"

The words had been like a red flag before a bull. I took up the challenge: not to beat him fair and square, as Uncle Albert had obviously intended for me to do, but to lose. He tried to let me win, exposing his king and queen, but I forced him into positions where he had to take my men, and I lost. Then I pouted. "I don't like this game. You said you were going to let me win."

He'd been so angry afterward that he could barely speak.

Aunt Patty hadn't set traps. Aunt Patty had imbued every act with hidden meaning. If I played with Lego it was, "What are you building?" "Why do you use all the red pieces first and then the yellow?" "Why does your house have so many windows? Are you afraid of being trapped in case of fire?" She'd been so sure she was onto something, I'd wanted to punch her.

I wasn't a bug to be dissected.

The memories made me dig my nails into my palms, and I stared blindly out the bus window. Through the trees I caught occasional glimpses of a lake. We were getting close to Three Hills, where the tournament was being held, a town of about five thousand that Mike and I had both lived in earlier. A museum town.

We didn't hit town until dark. In all the moving my family had done, I had yet to enter a town in full daylight. Either it was dark or I'd inexplicably fallen asleep en route.

Once at the hotel, Coach ordered us all to bed. I was assigned to share a room with Amy and her mother, who had come along as a chaperon.

Amy's mother snored, but that wasn't why I couldn't sleep. Every time I closed my eyes I saw the gold medal again: 2089.

Silently I got up and stole through the moonlight to stand by the mirror in my Mickey Mouse nightshirt. I pressed my cheek against the cool, silvered glass and traced designs with my finger. I hate you, I wrote on my reflection. Hate you, hate you, hate you.

CHAPTER

8

WE MET THE COMPETITION at breakfast the next day.

The hotel staff had put on a buffet in the banquet room for the tournament players. Mike and I had barely sat down after loading up our plates, when a boy and girl approached.

"May we join you?" The girl didn't wait for an answer, smoothly sitting down. "I'm Leona Cole, and this is my brother, Vincent. We play doubles for Three Hills. How about you?"

"Doubles for Chinchaga. I'm Mike, and this is Angel." Mike sounded friendly, but his gaze was cool.

So this was the competition.

Leona struck me as the leader of the two. I wondered if she and Vincent were twins. They resembled each other only slightly. Leona had a fox face while Vincent's was square. Her brown hair was drawn back in a cute ponytail, and she looked immaculate and at ease in tennis whites. She had dark striking eyebrows that winged upward like Mr. Spock's and a sharp, pointy chin.

"Angel Eastland and Michael Vallant? I recognize your names from some of the trophies," Leona said.

The mention of trophies and the hidden resentment in her tone made me look up sharply. Her eyes were violet.

My gaze snapped over to Vincent. He smiled at me deliberately. His eyes were violet, too.

I kicked Mike's ankle under the table to see if he'd noticed. He nudged me back. He had.

The Coles' reason for joining us soon became clear. They were there to psych us out. Leona managed to point out in casual conversation that, although they were younger than Mike and me, this was their second time at Zones, while it was our first. She jumped up at the end of the meal. "Excuse me, I have to say hello to Oliver and Jasmine. Oliver's hilarious—he had me in stitches at Zones last year."

Vincent excused himself and followed, his heavy-lidded gaze lingering on me for a moment. Flirting.

"Well, well," I said under my breath. With so many voices talking at once I didn't feel in danger of being overheard. "Did you catch that? Leona and Vincent."

"Leonardo da Vinci," Mike said at once.

I nodded. "Yes. And we must be Michelangelo. Michael and Angel."

Leonardo da Vinci and Michelangelo were both well-known Renaissance figures. *Renaissance* meant "rebirth," I remembered.

Renaissance must have been a code word. I wondered how many other teenage survivors of the Orphanage fire there were running around with matched names. Was there a Nicola and a Mac, for Niccolò Machiavelli? A Mona and a Lisa?

And Leona and Vincent obviously had the same idea we did: win Zones, go on to Provincials in Lethbridge, and escape.

Only one pair could win. I was determined that it would be us. Leona and Vincent would just have to wait until next year.

Mike and I had come prepared to play hard to win, and the caliber of the opponents we faced that day was something of a letdown. Most were mediocre. Only a few came up to the level of Kyle and Amy. After annihilating our first two opponents we relaxed enough to have a little fun.

When I became involved in a volley, taking ten shots in a row, Mike threw up his arms and appealed to the crowd about the unfairness of it all. He wandered off to the side of the court and tied his shoe, then took a drink of water, while I was forced to run to all corners of the court to keep the birdie in play. The crowd loved it, and I eventually "persuaded" Mike to help me play again.

Afterward Coach Hrudey frowned at us but didn't scold. His attention was focused on the match Leona and Vincent were playing. "They're your competition," he said.

I was not surprised.

"Individually they're very good, but they don't play well as a team. Their coach should enter them in singles play, not mixed doubles," Coach gave his professional opinion. He harrumphed. "But then I've never heard of their coach before. I'd swear he doesn't know one end of the racket from the other."

There were no playoffs, except in case of a tie. The team with the best record after round-robin play took home a trophy.

Through some "coincidence," Mike and I were scheduled to play Leona and Vincent last on Sunday morning. On Saturday night both our teams had perfect records.

Coach didn't want to let Mike and me go to the dance that night in the gym, but the two of us wore him down. All the nets had been taken down and cleared away, though no one had gone so far as to put up streamers. A live band called the Kinetic Yankees provided the music. They were dressed almost exactly like the Bon Jovi posters Wendy had hung on her wall, but they played a selection of pop rock mixed in with some old Beatles tunes.

They weren't bad, but they were trying too hard. All that hair flinging looked rehearsed.

It struck me again, like a bullet in the back. Of course it was rehearsed. They were playing music that was over one hundred years old—classic rock.

I looked more closely at the other kids dancing. How giggly and enthusiastic they were, like people at a Halloween party admiring everyone else's innovative costumes.

The walls began to close in on me, trapping me. I felt smothered in smoke, a prisoner of the Orphanage fire again.

"Guess who's heading our way," Mike said softly. "Ready to divide and conquer?" He got up and asked Leona to dance as she approached. They moved onto the dance floor before I could protest that it looked to me as if Leona and Vincent were doing the conquering.

Vincent sat down beside me. "Up for the match tomorrow? I saw you and Mike play this afternoon. You looked good."

"Thanks. Our coach is a slave driver."

He laughed, but the sound rang false, as if the last thing he really felt like doing was laughing. "All coaches must be alike. Ours carries a whip."

I decided to try some psyching out of my own. "Yeah, just because Coach Hrudey won a championship way back when, he thinks his method is the only way."

Vincent didn't respond as I had expected him to. Instead of bragging about how many championships his own coach had won, he leaned forward, his face intense. "Is there an Erin Reinders living in Chinchaga?"

I blinked. "Not that I know of."

"She's very petite," Vincent said. "She has black hair and blue eyes. She—" Vincent suddenly shut up.

I looked over my shoulder and saw Mike and Leona walking toward our table, laughing. I felt a spurt of jealousy but controlled it. Mike was doing the same thing as I: gathering information.

"Mike," I said, "do you know an Erin Reinders? Vincent's looking for her."

Mike shook his head. "Sorry, no."

Leona looked daggers at Vincent. Whoever Erin Reinders was, Leona didn't want her anywhere near her brother. "If Erin wanted you to know where she was, she would have left you her bleeding address," she said sharply.

Vincent looked sullen, not abashed.

"I know a Heather Reinders," I lied. "If you like I could ask her if she knows an Erin—"

"Angel," Leona interrupted, her voice as sweet as syrup, "your skirt is ripped. You should go sew it up."

"Thanks," I said through clenched teeth. But when I looked at the hem in the washroom it was fine.

My hands stilled. Sew it up. And hadn't Leona said something earlier about being kept in stitches? Sewing. Stitches. I felt again the impact of the sewing machine against my shin, the wild cartwheel down the stairs. Did she know about the sewing machine? But how could she? She and Vincent were prisoners, just as Mike and I were.

Weren't they?

I mentioned my speculations to Mike during another one of our whisper-and-kisses conversations.

Mike disagreed. "She's just trying to bug you. The stitches comment was a coincidence."

"So did you learn much while you were dancing?"

He shrugged. "Just that they've been living here for three years. Leona had a few questions of her own."

"Like what?"

"She asked about you, actually. How long I had known you, that sort of thing."

"Do you think we should tell them?" I asked. "About 2089?"

"No."

Mike's swift answer troubled me because I felt the same way. "In the Orphanage the doctors encouraged us to compete against one another," I reminded him. "That's part of why it took us so long to get together. Do we really want to keep doing what the doctors want us to?"

Mike took more time to answer the second time, but still shook his head. "We don't know the Coles well enough to trust them. Besides, they may already know."

"They're very quick," I agreed.

Mike kissed my nose. "But not as quick as we are."

I wasn't quite so sure the next morning. Leona seemed plenty quick to me as she drove the shuttlecock toward my face. My return shot wasn't high enough, and the birdie got stuck in the net. Since it had been their serve they got the point, putting them in the lead, 3–1.

The crowd cheered. Leona and Vincent were

the home favorites, but the constant roar made me feel grim.

Mike's backhand won us the serve back. After that, service kept switching without anyone making a point. The crowd's roar grew. Two other matches were in progress, but the crowd focused solely on us. They booed when I finally smashed one down the center to score a point.

The center turned out to be Leona and Vincent's weak spot. Coach was right: they played side by side like individual singles players not used to sharing a court, whereas Mike and I had grown almost into a single unit under Coach's drilling. We could play side by side, front and back, or rotation as we pleased. Usually in mixed doubles the girl played front and the guy in back. Mike and I could play either way.

We pulled ahead 7–5.

Each point was hotly contested, averaging around forty shots in a single rally. The sweat rolled off our bodies. Leona's face showed her true aggressiveness, teeth bared, eyes glaring. She and Vincent pushed themselves to the limit, stretching to reach those impossible shots and sometimes doing it. They drove the score back up to 12–11, in their favor.

We were like gladiators fighting, and the losers would get thrown to the lions.

Every muscle in my body ached, but I was not about to lose this game. I raced to return a drive from Vincent. I wound up as if I was going to clear; then I pulled back, just tipping the birdie over onto the other side. Leona scrambled for it but missed, falling to her knees on the court.

The crowd roared unhappily.

Our point, making it 12–12. I had just served when something hit me between the shoulder blades. A soda pop can. Vincent smashed the shuttlecock down the center. I pointed out the pop can to the ref, but he didn't return service to us. Coach looked as if he was about to have a fit.

I was a little shaken, and Vincent and Leona concentrated their shots on me like wolves scenting blood. The score was 13–12, their favor.

"Do you really think it will be that easy?" Leona asked mockingly. "To escape?"

Any lingering thought of collaboration and cooperation with the Coles left me then. Mike and I *would* win.

Mike correctly judged that a birdie would fall out of bounds and won us back service. He sent the shuttlecock winging over the net. Vincent was tiring—his shot had little zing—but I still stumbled over my feet returning it. We won the point, to the disappointment of the crowd.

It was 13–13.

I limped gingerly back to my usual position.

Leona and Vincent saw, conferred, and elected not to reset the score back to zero.

"Are you okay?" Mike asked before serving.

I winked at him.

Sure enough, Vincent's first shot was to the far left corner, intending to make me run on my sore ankle. I leaped up and smashed the birdie down between Leona's feet. "Na-na-na-na-na," I sang softly. Rage at being conned swept over her face.

I barely heard the catcalls from the crowd. It was 14–13 for us.

I grinned nastily, then served my best backhand with the top of my racket instead of the bottom. The birdie skimmed across the net, flat and fast, then dropped like a rock. Leona lunged forward to get it. The tip thwacked against her racket—

And a gunshot cracked out.

The bullet ricocheted off the net post, and simultaneously the gym was plunged into darkness.

CHAPTER

9

THE INSTANT THE LIGHTS went out, Mike seized my hand and we ran for the door. The crowd was silent for a moment, shocked, wondering who had been shot; then a child screamed, and, as one animal, they stampeded.

Two more gunshots barked overhead. "Kill them!" someone screamed. "They're getting away!"

It was like running through a nightmare. People pushing and shoving everywhere, a human tide, screaming and crying. Hands grabbed at my arms, my legs. Mike fell once and was almost sucked down. I yanked him back to his feet with strength born of panic.

Someone had thrown open the doors, shedding cloudy light on the mass of humanity. Mike and I were at the forefront of the wave, but not the first. The pressure from behind created a terrible bottleneck as everyone strove to reach the light, to reach safety.

A man yelled himself hoarse, exhorting every-one to stay calm and not panic. A few might have listened, but the gun blasted again, destroying all reason.

The crowd ripped Mike's hand from me. It was either let go or have my arm broken.

A surge from behind popped me through the door like a cork from a bottle.

Dim sunlight. Air.

I gasped in a few breaths, looking desperately for Mike, but the crowd kept pushing me forward. Pavement scuffed under my running shoes.

Once outside, the people milled around uncertainly. I stayed with them, just one more blond in a sea of them. I realized I was still hold-ing my badminton racket and dropped it imme-diately. I couldn't do much about the distinctive white top and short skirt.

A few smarter people ran for their cars and screeched out of the parking lot.

I thought that was an excellent idea: escape in the pandemonium before the shooter found me. The bullet had whipped within inches of my head. Someone had tried to kill me.

A flood of people spilled out the fire doors. I kept watching for a dark head. Where was Mike?

"Hurry." A strange man in a red jacket grabbed my arm. "This way."

I turned, ready to twist free, but saw Mike over his shoulder. He'd gotten out ahead of me somehow. The stranger pulled me in Mike's direction, and I didn't resist.

I thought Mike might know the muscled blond man, but the questioning look he flashed at me when we joined him told me he did not. I shook my head. I didn't know who he was either.

"This way," the stranger said. "My van's parked over here."

Mike shrugged, and we followed, swerving through the running crowd like separate strands of hair being braided together.

"My name's Dave Belcourt," the man said when we reached his navy blue van. He shook Mike's hand, then mine. "Your coach has told me a lot about you. I represent Nike running shoes. We're interested in signing you up to be spokespersons for our company."

It would be just like Coach to try to drum up sponsors before we'd even won our first tournament.

"Get us out of here, and we'll talk," Mike said.

Dave grinned. He was in his twenties, but the grin brought out a pair of dimples and made him look like a kid. "It's a deal." He slid open the van door, and we piled inside.

Mike sat in the back while I sat in the front seat with Dave.

"Can you believe this?" Dave said as he nosed forward into the parking lot, honking his horn to avoid running people down. "It's a riot."

"It's insane," I agreed.

We turned out of the parking lot onto the street. Escape beckoned just ahead.

"I've heard of hometown fanatics, but that

was crazy," Dave said. "I mean, to actually *shoot* at one of the contestants . . ." He shook his head.

I shivered, and it wasn't all faked. "I won't feel safe until we get out of this town."

"I don't blame you a bit," Dave said fervently. "Shall we just drive around for about fifteen minutes? I can tell you some more about Nike while we wait for things to cool down." Dave signaled, and we turned down a secondary road just within town limits that said "Agricultural Hall 5 km."

Mike and I exchanged quick glances in the mirror. I nodded slightly and started asking Dave questions about his Nike ad campaign while Mike unobtrusively searched the back of the van.

Dave seemed to be a cheerful individual and talked my ear off for the next ten miles about how he'd gotten an idea for a commercial while watching us on the court. "We'll start out with a shot of all that footwork, twisting and turning and leaping . . ."

I kept an eye on the mirror but did not see one vehicle in pursuit. Good.

Mike touched my arm; I took that as my signal. I screamed.

Dave slammed on the brakes. "What the hell?"

"A body." I was already scrambling out of my seat belt. "There was a body in the ditch." I threw open my door and jumped out.

"Are you sure?" Dave followed me doubtfully. "Maybe it was just a garbage bag or—"

Mike leaped on his shoulder, tackling him down onto the highway. Dave was big and strong enough to pose for athletic commercials himself, but the move knocked the wind out of him. Before he could recover, I stood by his head. "Make one move and I'll kick your skull in."

He went very still. "What—the hell—are you doing?"

"Hush, now. We'll have plenty of time to chat later." Mike pressed his knee into Dave's back. He swiftly bound Dave's hands together with a length of rope he must have found in the back, then patted Dave down for weapons.

"Are you robbing me? My wallet's in my back pocket."

"Good idea," I said. Mike handed it to me, and I put it in my skirt pocket to examine later. "Now get up."

Painfully, Dave rolled onto his knees on the pavement. His chin was scraped and bruised, and he got up slowly.

"Into the van," Mike said.

"I don't under—" In midsentence Dave pivoted, kicking his leg straight out at the right height to catch Mike painfully on the chin, but Mike wasn't there anymore. He ducked out of range, and I kicked Dave in the back of the knee, buckling his other leg.

Mike and I surveyed him on the ground. "Some people are just slow learners." Mike shook his head sadly.

"Real slow," I agreed, but my confidence was

an act. Inside, my heart was trying to beat its way out of my chest.

Sullenly, Dave got up. We strapped him into one of the back seats in the van and tied his feet together. He kept up his innocent act. "Why are you doing this? I was trying to help you. Nike would have paid you millions."

We ignored him. Mike climbed into the driver's seat and put the van in gear. We couldn't afford to sit here much longer. Sooner or later traffic would come by.

"Where were you taking us?" I asked.

Dave looked bewildered. He really was very good. "Nowhere. I was just driving around."

"You can cut the act," Mike told him. "You gave yourself away just after we left the parking lot."

"I don't know what you're talking about, I swear to God. Please, I have a wife and a little girl at home. Her name is Cindy."

I winced. "Going a little over the top, aren't we?" I pulled out his wallet and flipped through the little plastic windows. "Funny, but I don't see any pictures of little girls in here." Dave was silent while I took out his driver's license. It really did say Dave Belcourt, and the photograph looked like him. They'd come prepared.

All the dates on the money were right, all of it pressed new as if it had just come out of a bank machine.

However, tucked inside one of the pockets I found something very interesting indeed: a plain white card with the name David Jared

Belcourt and a twenty-digit number. It was made of hard plastic like a credit card, but it was thicker, made of two layers held together by a tiny screw. "Is there anything here to crack it open with?" I asked Mike.

Dave started to protest, then caught himself.

"There should be something in the toolbox under the seat."

I found a thin-bladed nail file and turned the tiny screw, opening it. I showed the inside to Mike in silence. It looked, from what I vaguely recalled from computer ads, like a silicon chip.

"What's this, Dave? Your identification? Your driver's license? Your bank account? Or all three?" I watched him carefully. He was sweating. "I think it's all three. What happens if I grind it to pieces, Dave? Do I wipe out your life savings?"

"What do you want?" he gritted.

"That's the spirit," Mike said. "We'd like to know why you and your friends just tried to kill us."

"What makes you think I had anything to do with that?" Dave tried one last bluff.

I ticked items off on my fingers. "The Nike story was clever but a little thin." Somehow I suspected Nike running shoes and the nature of commercials would have changed in some form over a hundred years. "Your van was parked with the nose pointing out for a fast getaway. You're wearing a jacket, while all the others inside the gym had taken theirs off because it was so hot. But the clincher was when you knew the gunman was shooting at us. Every other panicked person inside was convinced the madman might shoot them next—which is why they ran. If you knew we were the targets, you should have stayed where it was safe, up in the stands, rather than risk the stampeding crowd below. So I think you were outside the whole time—the backup, in case we escaped."

Dave's expression changed. "You supercilious little bastards. *Homo sapiens* effing *renascentia*. The scientists can't shield you forever. You'll burn in end, just like the others. They smelled like pork."

Mike stepped forward as if to hit Dave, but I stopped him. Dave's taunts about the Orphanage fire weren't important. The rest of what he was saying was.

"He'll get you," Dave vowed. "He's smarter than both of you put together."

"Who is?" I asked.

Dave clamped his mouth shut after that, but he'd already told us more than I would ever have guessed on my own.

Homo sapiens renascentia, not *Homo sapiens sapiens.*

Renascentia was Latin for "renaissance," which meant rebirth and renewal. Not a new species but a new subspecies.

Homo sapiens sapiens were current humankind. The Cro-Magnons were the first *sapiens sapiens* to appear, 35,000 years ago. *Homo sapiens neanderthalensis* had been the Neanderthals. Depending on which theory you subscribed to,

Neanderthals had either been assimilated by the Cro-Magnons or killed off by the Cro-Magnons. Off with the old, on with the new. Survival of the fittest.

The endless tests made sense now. So did the attack. Apparently some people, like Dave, felt threatened by us.

"An interesting story, Dave m'boy," Mike said in a jocular British accent. "Also, a crock of manure. We're no less human than you are."

I stared at him. Did he really not believe we were a different subspecies? Or had I missed something important?

I'd missed something. I followed Mike's gaze to the rearview mirror where a police car rode on our tail. We'd taken about five turns at random. They shouldn't have been able to find us so fast.

Unless there was a tracking device on the van.

Which meant Dave wasn't a terrorist; he was in league with the scientists. This had been their plan from the beginning. All the gunshots and screaming—that was just a bunch of extras hired for a movie, intended to flush out our true nature with real danger.

I remembered Leona's mocking words: "Do you really think it will be that easy to escape?" Had she somehow known what would happen?

We'd blown it.

Swearing under his breath, Mike pulled over, and we waited for the cops.

CHAPTER

10

THINGS WENT DECEPTIVELY well—at first.

I'd been sure the scientists would haul us away to some compound, but instead the cops arrested Dave as one of the terrorists, and Mike and I were sent home on the bus with Coach Hrudey, who was still upset over the tournament being called a tie. To his credit, I don't think he realized the gunman had been shooting at us. Mike and I both fell asleep on the bus—a sedative in the air, not in the food, as I had made sure not to eat or drink anything—and woke up in Chinchaga. I slept in my own bed that night as usual.

When I woke the next morning I still couldn't believe Mike and I had gotten away with it. Before the blow fell, I felt wary but also energized.

Our continuing freedom raised a lot of interesting possibilities. Maybe it had been a coincidence that the cops had found Dave's van so quickly. Maybe the van had had a tracking device but no bugs. Maybe the scientists were playing some deeper game.

I was eager to discuss everything with Mike on our morning run, but when I went outside, Mike wasn't there.

I looked at my watch, saw that I was five minutes early, and jogged over to Mike's house, figuring I'd meet him halfway, but I didn't encounter him.

I stood outside on the dewy grass and threw pebbles at his window. There was no response. The blind was down, so I assumed he was still asleep, fighting off the effects of the scientists' sedatives.

Vaguely concerned, I rang the doorbell, a rude thing to do at seven-thirty in the morning, but I didn't care. Although Mom and Dad were now behaving like newlyweds, I still harbored a lingering hostility toward Mr. Vallant.

Mrs. Vallant finally opened the door, wearing a black negligee and a matching peignoir. "Yes?" She didn't sound as though she was in a very good mood.

A faint alarm began to ring in my brain as I pushed past her. "Hi," I said cheerfully. "I'm here to collect Mike. We're supposed to go for a run this morning."

She crossed her arms, a look of sullen triumph on her face. "I'm afraid that's not possible. Mike's not here."

My heart began to beat harder. "Where is he?"

She smiled maliciously. "Why, dear, didn't he tell you? He received special acceptance to the university two weeks ago. He left on a one o'clock flight last night."

"Ah," I said softly, as if my whole world hadn't just crashed down around me. The scientists had taken Mike; I didn't believe for a moment her implication that Mike had gone willingly.

"I loaned him a book. Do you mind if I take a look in his room for it?" It wasn't really a question, since I didn't wait for an answer. I zigzagged around her and dashed down the hallway and into Mike's room.

She trailed after me, her voice falsely sweet. "Oh, dear, I've upset you, haven't I? I hope you weren't serious about Michael. I'm afraid he's a bit of a flirt. You're not the first girl to cry over him."

The enjoyment on her face made me feel sick.

Mike's bed was messy, but I couldn't tell if Mike had slept in it or just not made it Friday morning. The closet was open and empty. His racket was jammed in a pile of dirty socks in the corner instead of in its wood press.

I picked out a Hardy Boys book from his shelf—*The Missing Chum*—and turned to leave the room. Mr. Vallant joined his wife in the hallway. In a burgundy robe, open to show his chest, he looked shady and disreputable. Despite the gray in his stubble he seemed to think he was pretty hot stuff. He ran his eyes over me like a measuring tape. "Hello there, pretty Angel. Say hello to your mother for me, will you? The firm's transferring us, and I might not see her again."

No word about his son, about Mike being packed off without warning.

I pictured how much nicer he would look with a black eye. "You didn't deserve him," I told them, slashing my gaze from one to the other. "Either of you."

I left the house at a dead run, chased by memories.

Sitting together on the bus ride home, sharing whispered secrets. "Tell me something about yourself nobody else knows," he'd said. "Anything."

So I'd told him how as a kid I'd loved the taste of strawberry ice cream, but I hated it now because I'd figured out they'd used the sweet taste to disguise the pills they were drugging me with and I'd been such a glutton I hadn't even noticed.

"Your turn," I said, smiling. "Tell me something you never told a living soul." I looped my arms around his neck.

"All right. Something I've never told anyone else, right?" he murmured in my ear. "Here goes: you're pulling my hair."

I squawked and gave his hair a good yank.

"What?" Mike said innocently. "I've never told that to a single soul."

I reached up to pull his hair again, and he kissed me, laughing. "Don't be dumb," I gasped at last. "Tell me something important: why did you pick such horrible parents?"

His good humor faded, and he stared off into the distance. "Because they're so unlikable. It'd be impossible to forget who they work for and become attached to them."

As I was attached to mine.

At home I flew up the stairs to my bedroom like an arrow released from a bow.

The white comforter, huge pillows, and scarred wooden dresser, which this morning had seemed so cozy, a haven, now appeared unbearably innocent to my eyes. Innocent and false, hiding the cancer at its heart.

I had a small desk and a chair, which I used more as a clothes hanger than as something to sit on. I swept the jeans aside, grabbed the back of the chair and swung it at the floor-to-ceiling mirror.

I caught a glimpse of myself in the glass just before the chair legs punched through and was surprised at how calm I looked. Perhaps a little pale, a little grim around the mouth, that was all.

The mirror fractured; isosceles triangles dropped like knives; powdered glass drifted down. A hundred small mirrors were born of one big one, and I saw a hundred avenging angels snarl and swing the chair again, grimness swallowed by savagery.

Glass sprayed everywhere, an explosion of crystal shards. I nicked my arms in a couple of places and received a cut above my left eyebrow, but I wouldn't have known it except for the blood dripping into my eyes.

I reached through the hanging jaws of glass to the shelf mounted inside the wall and seized the camera that had spied on me all these months. The thickness of the wall had alerted me to the camera's presence soon after we moved to Chinchaga, but at the time it had been in my best interests to play dumb and pretend it wasn't there. Now I threw it out the window to the hard ground below.

My parents burst into the room. Their alarm grew when they saw the glass carpet at my feet, sparkling on my hair and clothes.

"Angel!" Mom reached for me, then drew back.

"Mike's gone," I said. My voice was stark, brutal.

An expression slithered behind their masks, too quick for me to read. "I'm sorry to hear that," Dad said. "He seemed like a nice young man. Whatever's happened, we can help you."

I cut him off before he could edge into "Why have you destroyed your room?"

"Am I your daughter?"

Their emotions swam closer to the surface. Shock? Pain?

"We meant to tell you," Mom said, rushing into a rehearsed speech.

"We should have told you earlier, but the time never seemed right." Dad sat down on the bed with a defeated sigh. "It's hard even to know where to start. With the basics, I guess. We adopted you when you were four years old."

"*No.* You're not listening to me." I stamped my foot, and glass slivers fell from my hair. "Am

I or am I not your daughter? Is Mom your wife or isn't she? Make a choice."

Silence.

Then Dad spoke, fiercely, "She is, by God. You're my daughter, and she's my wife, and no two-bit weasel is going to take her away." He swept the two of us into a hug on the glass-sprinkled floor.

Mom was crying.

I got the whole story from them in bits and pieces.

They'd fallen in love at university. Both of them had majored in drama. In their time all education from kindergarten to postdoctoral studies was provided free by the government, but once you graduated—or if you flunked out once too often—they demanded repayment. Instead of having to pay back student loans, you owed them several years of your life working on government projects.

"We applied for a family license," Mom said, "but they wouldn't give us one until our years were paid up."

"There's not a lot of government work for actors," Dad said, "and we were faced with doing data entry and janitorial work at opposite ends of the country. It would have taken us five and a half years to get out of debt, and even then there was no guarantee that our application to marry would be accepted."

"So when the offer came along—"

"—to come here and pretend to be a family—"

"—and have a sweet little girl of our own"—

they exchanged glances—"we jumped at it," Dad finished.

"It was only supposed to be for three years." Mom closed her eyes, sitting on the edge of my bed. "And at the end we'd be all paid up."

"With a bonus to equal the rest if they got the desired results early," Dad added.

"After we mastered the history requirements it was easy. All that money for acting like a family, which was all we wanted to be anyhow. And when you were at school we could do whatever we liked. Take watercolor painting—" Mom's eyes misted.

"—stage little theater productions. It was no hardship to be your parents, Angel."

"We loved you," Mom said.

Dad sighed. "So when they offered to extend the contract for real money for another five years or as long as it took, we accepted."

"There were things we shut our eyes to," Mom admitted. "Things we shouldn't have allowed."

"Whenever we moved to a new house we would gradually realize there were more cameras, more listening devices, more reports to fill out than at the last place as they became more and more desperate." Heaviness filled Dad's voice, and he could not look at me. He kept staring at the broken mirror.

"But by then we were in so deep—"

"—and they kept blackmailing us, dangling that damned family license in front of our face—"

"—and we didn't want to leave you, Angel. You're part of our hearts now."

"We thought, At least we love her. At least we can protect her from them a little." Dad looked pained. "These last two months have been absolute hell."

"That horrible Mr. Vallant." Mom shuddered. "At first it was just 'Flirt with him. Mike and Angel will unite forces to break you two up.' Then when that didn't work they came up with that awful marriage scheme. 'You can still be together during the day,' they said."

Dad put an arm around her shoulders. "We'd just decided we couldn't go through with it when you and Mike started dating."

Mom looked up, concern for me plain in her expression. "We knew right away he wasn't one of your regular boyfriends. We've been so worried for you, darling."

Mike was gone. Fear slammed into me like a wall of water, poured through me, hollowing me out inside. What would I do if he was gone forever? "Do you know where they've taken him?"

Mom shook her head. "Somewhere outside town, I'm sure. They don't tell us any more than they have to."

"They know whose side we're on," Dad said softly.

I swallowed past a lump in my throat the size of a golf ball and hugged them both again. "I chose well when I was four."

"What are you going to do now?" Dad asked.

Get Mike back. "Declare war. Do me a favor?"

"Anything," Mom said passionately.

"Disable the rest of the bugs."

Dad was already nodding. "Can do. What about you?"

I flashed them a tight smile. "It's eight-thirty, time to go to school." I had more questions—dozens of them—but after smashing the mirror I didn't dare remain in one place for very long. At least not until I was dealing from a position of strength.

I figured that if the scientists could still hear me, they would think I was going anywhere but school—so that's where I went.

Wendy looked surprised when I tapped on the window at the back corner of the math room, but she didn't hesitate to open it. "Late again, Angel? Hurry up before Mr. Thrombel arrives."

I shook my head. "You come out here. I need to talk to you."

Wendy shrugged and immediately started wiggling her way out the window.

Some of the other kids laughed, but they quieted down when I put a finger to my lips. They wouldn't give us away to Mr. Thrombel, expecting some kind of joke. But it wasn't a joke this time, and I just hoped that whatever candid camera had been set up didn't cover the back corner, or that the technician had gone for a coffee break and missed it.

Wendy somersaulted onto the lawn beside me. "If I get grass stains on my new jeans you're dead," she groused.

I wasn't listening. "Come on. I don't want anyone to see us." I pulled her to her feet, urging her up the wooded hill behind the football field.

"Here," Wendy said when we finally stopped. "Have a Kit Kat finger." She snapped me off a piece of slightly melted chocolate bar.

I stared at it blankly.

"You haven't heard the news yet, have you?" She grinned, exhilarated. "I'm handing out candy instead of cigars. Raven had the baby Friday night—Saturday, really, at four o'clock in the morning. Eight pounds, thirteen ounces. He's perfect, as fat and healthy as a tick. They're naming him Dimitri. Dad stayed home today on paternity leave because they're bringing the baby home from the hospital. I said, Hey, what about sorority leave? Don't sisters have any rights? But they made me come to school anyhow. Do you want to come home with me at noon and—"

I cut off the flood. "Mike's gone."

It took a few seconds for my words to penetrate. "Gone where? Did you two win the tournament?"

We'd lost very badly. "He's gone. His mother says he got early acceptance to the university, but she's lying. He's been kidnapped," I said starkly.

"Kidnapped? Why? I mean, Mike's not rich or anything, is he? Maybe his aunt died, and he had to leave town or something. He'll be back in a couple of days."

"The only relatives Mike has are Uncle Albert and Aunt Patty, same as me."

Wendy blinked. "You and Mike are cousins?"

"Not exactly," I said impatiently. I didn't have time to explain. "Mike didn't leave for a funeral. He's in trouble." The words sounded woefully inadequate. The scientists had taken him at one o'clock this morning. Hours ago. "Please, Wendy, just take my word for it. Mike's in trouble, and I need your help."

Her expression turned serious. "Shoot."

I paced restlessly. "I need to know where we are—exactly where we are. All I have are guesses based on tiny scraps of knowledge."

"What do you mean? We're in Chinchaga."

"Where's Chinchaga? In Canada, like we've been told? Does Canada still exist? Are we in Alberta? Or the United States? We could be in Russia for all I know."

Wendy stared. "Is this some kind of test? I know I said I wouldn't care if my dad got fined last time, but I was a little surprised when you reported me."

"It's not a test, and I didn't report you. Until you mentioned it, I didn't even know there were fines." She was still staring. How could I convince her? Time was so short. "Please, Wendy. Pretend I really am from 1987, that I've been locked in a time capsule and never allowed outside all the museums. *Where are we?*"

"Okay," she said softly. "You can laugh at me later. We're in Chinchaga, Peace River Province. The location on the maps is pretty accurate. Canada still exists as part of the larger North American Community."

I took in a deep breath. "And what is Chinchaga?"

She still hesitated.

"I've been living in these museum towns since I was four years old," I said. "I know why I'm here and why Mike was here, but why are all the rest of you here?"

She still looked as if she couldn't decide whether I was lying or not. "Everyone has different reasons. Carl's a Spacer; his parents sent him here to avoid the war. He's on a scholarship. Maryanne's parents are antique collectors. My dad's an archaeology professor, and he and Raven thought a change of scene might be best for me. Get me away from all my city friends." A fleeting smile touched her mouth. "I'm surprised they didn't change their minds and yank me out of here when I started dating Carl. But the fees are nonrefundable, of course."

I felt like strangling her. "Fees for what? What is this place?"

"Historical Immersion class. You know, 'Don't just study the past, live it.' "

I went very still, more pieces tumbling into place.

"They're springing up all over," Wendy chattered. "Historical Immersions and Historical Reenactments of the Old West, China at the time of Genghis Khan—Egypt is very popular—the Second World War, Watergate. I wanted the 1960s—the Bay of Pigs, Apollo Eleven, and all that—but Dad held out for the beginning of the computer age and the fall of the Berlin Wall in

1989, and of course Raven voted with him. . . ." My expression seemed to sink in. Wendy's mouth, outlined in dark red lipstick, fell open. "You didn't know. You *really* didn't know."

I clutched a tree for support, eyes closed, bark digging into the soft flesh of my palms. "Wendy, I don't even know what *year* this is."

"It's 2098."

That was 111 years after 1987. My mind raced. If the scientists' purpose had been to retard us technologically, why hadn't they pushed us back even further? Made us serfs under the whip of the tsar in Russia, for instance?

The answer surfaced at once: there were no schools back then. The scientists wanted to test our intelligence, so they needed a time period where most people finished high school and went on to college.

"No wonder you never slipped," Wendy whispered. "Who did this to you?"

Time to gamble. "Remember the social studies test I got ninety-eight on? I can get one hundred on any test I want, without studying, if I've seen the material even once."

She squinted at me through a thick coating of mascara. "So you're, like, some kind of genius?"

I nodded. "The scientists figure we're some kind of new human subspecies. *Homo sapiens renascentia.* They want to study us, use us. Another group wants to kill us." Dave had turned out to be a fake, but the Orphanage fire had been all too real.

"Bizarre." Wendy shook her head.

"Do you believe me?"

"Hey, I've seen some of your schemes in action. I always told Dad you were smarter than you made out."

"Good. Will you help me?"

"Of course."

I looked her straight in the eye. "It might mean more than a few fines this time. You'll be going against the government."

She grinned recklessly. "According to local law I'm still a minor. How bad can it be?"

"Bad."

Wendy raised a thinly plucked eyebrow. "Are you going to tell me the plan or not?"

"Who said I had a plan?"

She laughed. "Angel, you always have a plan. You'll break Mike out with a flamethrower and a bucket of water if you have to."

So I told her.

She gave a low whistle when I finished. "Sounds like fun."

So we went back down the hill and caused a riot.

CHAPTER

11

WE SET EVENTS IN MOTION by barging into our math class. Mr. Thrombel looked annoyed but resigned. He waved us to our seats.

I didn't take mine. "Mr. Thrombel, can you help me with a small math problem?"

"What is it?" Mr. Thrombel was a fairly relaxed teacher and could often be steered off the curriculum into digressions.

"I was just looking in the hallway, and I could swear the outside of this room is bigger than the inside. I mean, I know the walls account for some of the difference, but it's off by quite a bit. Come see."

Mr. Thrombel loved to bite into a good, practical math problem. He produced measuring tapes from his desk and got half the class to measure the inside of the room while the remaining half measured the outside.

To Mr. Thrombel's consternation the inside of

the math room *was* too small by several square feet.

"Hypotheses, class?"

"We measured wrong?" Maryanne suggested.

"That might account for an inch or two, but not four feet," he said.

"The inside walls are thicker than the walls we measured?" someone proposed.

"A distinct possibility, but a four-foot-thick wall does seem a little odd." Mr. Thrombel worried over the problem.

"Maybe there's a secret passageway," I said. Before he could point out how unlikely that was, I added, "How would you find out if there was one?"

"Look for secret doors, I suppose," he said.

"Let's do it," I said, projecting my excitement at the rest of the class like a lantern throwing out light.

Mr. Thrombel frowned mildly. "We're supposed to be learning trigonometry."

The class groaned in unison.

He grinned. "On the other hand, I never could resist a mystery."

I remembered why Mr. Thrombel was my favorite teacher, and I hoped he wouldn't get into too much trouble when this blew up in his face.

The wall was constructed of concrete, patterned to resemble stone and painted white. While the rest of the class prodded at the baseboards and the corners—"Someone should dust a little more often. Phew!" Maryanne said—

Wendy and I stood on desks and attacked the chalkboard.

A metal bracket in each corner kept it attached to the wall.

Fortunately, I had thought ahead and borrowed a screwdriver from the janitor's closet earlier. Wendy had taken a battery-operated electric screwdriver on the principle that if you were going to steal something, you might as well steal the best.

Mine took longer, but it was quieter. Half the class looked up when she unscrewed the bolts on her side. I slipped the bracket in my pocket then lifted the chalkboard out of the bottom bracket. The thing was heavy. "Timber," I cried, jumping from my desk.

The chalkboard crashed to the floor.

The effect was even more dramatic than I'd hoped. Some advanced technology had allowed the scientists to treat the chalkboard like a two-way mirror. There was a big hole where the board had been, a three-foot crawlway equipped with cameras, and we had a picture-window view of Mrs. Jamison's English class.

A stunned silence descended.

Maryanne broke it. "Holy crow."

"We're being spied on," Mr. Thrombel said. There was a restrained horror in his voice. I remembered that he had gotten married just a few months ago.

I wondered if alarms were going off at the scientists' headquarters yet. "It's filming us right now. Cover it up!"

Two nylon backpacks did the trick quite nicely.

As per orders Wendy slipped out the door and over to Mrs. Jamison's class. They had all heard the crash. I watched through the hole behind the chalkboard while the math class buzzed.

I couldn't hear Wendy's voice, but whatever she said worked. Mrs. Jamison left the room. Carl was in the class, and when he got up to follow Wendy, a few other people drifted out into the hallway.

Mrs. Jamison came into the math classroom and put a hand to her throat, blinking in surprise at the sight of the camera port. Apparently none of the teachers had known; I was pleased my gamble had paid off.

When two-thirds of the English class had crowded into the math room I made a discovery. "Hey, look! There are ladder rungs on the inside of the wall." A row of them marched up beside the space where the chalkboard had hung.

Mr. Thrombel had long since lost control of his students; within minutes, Carl, Wendy, and a couple of other boys had climbed up the ladder to take a look. I stayed below to keep an eye on the situation.

Mrs. Jamison was just on the point of ordering her class back to their room when Jimmy came back down the ladder, face red with excitement. "You won't believe this, but there's an entire attic up there."

From outside, the small peak to the school's roof looked large enough only for a small crawl space. The builders must have lowered the classroom ceiling a bit and added in a few extra feet of wall between the inner ceiling and the outer roof.

"There are ladders and hidden cameras between *all* the classrooms and even one by the principal's office!" Jimmy continued. "There's a whole room full of TV monitors up there showing the whole school!"

About fifteen more people had to go up to believe, but I took his word for it. Spying weasels. It was all going to backfire in the scientists' faces this time. I moved on to the next step.

"Let's go tell the other classes!" I yelled.

After that it was routine. Take down the chalkboards. Cover up the cameras. Spread the word to the next class. Send a few people up the ladders to report their findings.

In an hour the whole school was milling chaos. Exactly how I wanted it.

The principal's office was empty, all the staff having left to find out what was going on, so it was a cinch to take over the P.A. system. I got Carl to make the announcement, since his voice was deep enough to pass for a teacher's. "May I have your attention, please? Would everyone in the school please go to the gymnasium? Repeat: everyone in the school, go to the gym. I don't have any more answers than you do, but we can figure this out together."

A secretary rushed back inside, furious that we weren't teachers, but I ignored her and disabled the mike so she couldn't correct the announcement.

Everyone was a little relieved at the hint of

possible explanations, and the students were happy and excited to be taking a break from school. They all went into the gym.

Are you watching, scientists? I wanted to yell, to scream. *Are you getting nervous yet? You should be. It's too big for you to stop now; the questions have all been raised. You can't stuff them back into Pandora's box.*

Are you sorry you took Mike?

You made a big mistake there, but it wasn't your biggest one. Your biggest mistake was leaving me behind.

The principal stood at the front of the crowd, trying to calm everyone down, but I vaulted to the stage behind him. At my signal Wendy flicked the lights off and back on. I'd learned something from Dave the Terrorist. Total darkness would have caused chaos, but flicking the lights just got the crowd's attention.

I raised my hands, and they fell silent as if by magic.

"I don't know about the rest of you, but I'm madder than hell," I said. "Somebody's been spying on us, listening to our every word, recording our every expression, and invading our privacy. Are you as mad as I am?"

"Yes!" the crowd yelled.

It was like working a pep rally. Not hard, really. I just let out all the anger I had felt three years ago when I realized there were cameras in my bedroom, where I undressed at night.

"They have no right to do this to us!" To me. "Are we criminals?"

"No!" howled the crowd.

"Did we deserve to be treated this way? Spied on, our secrets pried into?"

"No!"

The principal climbed onto the stage, hands held out placatingly. "You're overreacting." He reminded the students what a privilege it was to be here, without actually saying where that was. How they had fought to be accepted into the "program." It was logical that the people in charge would want some record of what happened; there was no need to be paranoid.

Then he made a slip. "Just because there are cameras in the school doesn't mean there are cameras in our homes."

The crowd hadn't even considered that possibility yet and muttered angrily.

My turn again. "There's a camera in my bedroom," I yelled. "There are cameras in yours, too!"

Which might or might not have been true, depending on how desperate the scientists were. Had the scientists wired only the houses of the people Mike and I were likely to visit, or all of the houses?

"There was a camera in my bedroom, too," Wendy yelled loyally, and the crowd roared in outrage, jelling into a mob.

I had deliberately not searched for cameras in the gym and sincerely hoped the scientists were getting an eyeful.

I had a weapon now, and I intended to use it.

I yelled, but the crowd was shouting too loud

and didn't hear me. I would have to act quickly to stay in control.

I signaled Wendy, and she flicked the lights off and on again. Even then it took several tries to get their attention.

The energy and anger radiating off the students was enormous, near the flash point. If I'd had a castle to storm I could have done it. But I didn't know where the scientists had taken Mike. A different kind of destruction was in order.

"Are we going to stand for this?" I yelled.

"No!"

"Are we going to keep quiet about this?"

"No!"

"Are we going to let them buy our silence, or are we going to shout our outrage to the world?"

"Shout it!" The walls reverberated with their echoes.

I hadn't had a chance to ask Wendy about newspapers and freedom of the press, but I knew that in 1987 a story like this could topple a government. I only hoped the same was true in 2098.

"Are we going to stay here and take this?"

"No!"

"Are we going to leave?" My voice was going hoarse, but I had them now. The power I was wielding frightened me a little even as I gloried in it. It occurred to me that Dave might have been right to be afraid of us. Since learning of Mike's disappearance, it had taken me less than three hours to raise a mob.

"Yes!"

"But what will we do first?"

My thoughts jumped straight from my brain into their mouths.

"Smash the cameras!"

"Break—"

"Destroy—"

"Crush—"

I heard the faint wail of sirens outside and loosed the mob on the town. "Then let's do it. Let's go! Go! Go!" I jumped off the stage. The crowd turned like a tide, thundering out the doors.

The police let them go. Even if they were in the scientists' pay and not just playing a role like everyone else, they could hardly open fire on a bunch of kids and teachers.

The crowd dispersed, going home to smash up the cameras, leave the town, and spread their story.

I had a feeling that Historical Immersion classes would be unpopular for a while.

I found Wendy and Carl still by the light switches. "I have a small project," I yelled across the stream of people. "Can you round up fifteen or so people to help?"

We ended up with eighteen kids, including me.

"Hey, where's your Siamese twin?" Maryanne asked. "Where's Mike?"

Gone from me. Cut off. Kidnapped. In the hands of the enemy.

I fought off the debilitating fear and twisted the truth into a tool. "Mike and I stumbled on one of the cameras last night. Some men caught

Mike and took him away in a van. I've been hiding out ever since. That's why Wendy crawled out the window to meet me this morning in math class." It was always a good idea to add one bit of truth to every lie. "I need your help to get him back." Bald truth.

"How?" Carl asked. His face showed little, but he stood as if ready to pulverize boulders to get to his friend.

"We need to offer them something of equal value. Something to trade. A hostage."

Wendy put an arm around her own neck and pointed a finger to her head like a gun. "If you need volunteers, I'm your man."

Her stunt broke the tension. I smiled. "Thanks, but I had something a little more breakable in mind. Something we could toss off the roof."

"Like what? Baseballs?"

I smiled my hundred-candle smile. "No. Antiques. National treasures that can never be replaced."

A slow grin spread over Wendy's face. "Stuff brimming with history."

"You got it." I clapped my hands together. "Let's go on a scavenger hunt. Take all the loot up to their monitoring station in the attic." We split up at a run.

I went with Wendy because her dad was an archaeology professor. Left to my own devices, I would probably have collected things of the approximate value of a plastic bow and arrow stamped "Made in Taiwan."

"Computers first," Wendy said. "The Apple II's in the lab are as scarce as hen's teeth. Dad started drooling when he saw them. They must have robbed all the museums in North America to get twenty working models."

Carl helped us haul the computers up into the attic. Along the way, Wendy and I stuffed our pockets with Bic pens, battery-operated calculators, and other such junk. Even rulers that had inches as well as centimeters marked on them were worth a fair amount. Sewing machines, electric typewriters, digital clocks, microwave ovens, Beta VCRs. All the things I'd grown up with, Wendy labeled "priceless," "rarer than rubies," "stuff Dad would sell his soul to own." Not all of it was real; some of the antiques were fakes or copies. All the clothing, for instance, was merely copied from old catalogs.

Within an hour we had a veritable treasure hoard.

"All right," I said, stepping over a keyboard. "Time to make our demands. Anyone who doesn't want to get arrested should leave now."

I thought Maryanne might break and leave, but she stood firm. "Don't worry, Angel. We'll get Mike back."

"They had no right to do this to us," Jimmy said—a long speech for him.

Nods of agreement. Nobody left.

I'd always thought of myself as a brilliant outsider, valuable only for my entertaining schemes, and my friends' loyalty touched my heart.

I had to blink back tears before moving over to

the monitors, which now showed either empty classrooms or the inside of someone's backpack. I tapped the screens. "Whoever monitors these computers must have a way to contact their home base. Who's good at electronics?"

Carl raised his hand.

"Good. See if you can get the head honcho on the line, will you?"

Carl nodded and got down to work, fingers blurring over the keyboard. I swiftly dispatched the rest of my troops: some began moving antiques near the holes in the floor where the various ladders led down so the antiques could be pushed down the drop at any time, others stood lookout at all four of the school's entrances and exits, the rest guarded the ladders from above. Once I finished giving orders, I returned and hovered over Carl's shoulder. I could make little sense of what I saw on the screen in front of him.

"Don't worry," Wendy told me. "I don't know what it means either. Carl's a hacking genius. Most Aug—" She broke off, and I politely didn't ask.

We waited.

Hang on, Mike, I'm coming.

CHAPTER

12

"BINGO," CARL SAID SOFTLY, twenty minutes later. "The feed is going to the local TV channel." Another five minutes of typing, then a small frown. "I can't trace it any farther.

"Then we'll start there," I said.

"Coming up."

Wendy and I crowded around him. A slightly digitized image appeared of a man in a lab coat slurping coffee. He didn't look as if he was working very hard, but then, how hard could it be to play tapes of old newscasts and *Three's Company* reruns every hour or so?

"Can he see us?" I asked.

"No. I covered up the camera when I first came up here." Carl frowned. "I'm not even sure he knows we're here. The transmission is piggy-backed on the TV feed, but it's not going to the TV station. It's going somewhere else."

"It'll have to do. Good work." Wendy and I prepared a few props, then gave Carl the nod.

"Going to picture and sound." Carl clicked some buttons.

"Hey, meathead," I said.

The tech slopped his coffee, staring around in all directions. He must have been facing a wall of TVs too.

"Yeah, you with the coffee." He looked up, and I waved at him. I didn't give him a chance to speak. "Do you know what this is?" I stepped back and let him see one of the Apple II computers. It was plugged in, and the cursor was blinking placidly.

"Do you know how much this is worth?"

He shook his head.

"Tell him, Wendy."

"It's one of only twenty working models in the world. The last one that went to auction sold for nine million dollars, and that was four years ago."

The figure awoke a gleam of greed in his eye.

I took one of the baseball bats we'd snitched from the gym and hit a home run on the monitor.

"What are you doing?" he shrieked.

I hit it again. The plastic casing around the central processing unit proved to be rather tough, so I opened it up and broke all the delicate circuitry boards.

His mouth was hanging open when I finished.

Maryanne and a few others looked shocked, too. They hadn't really believed I would do it.

But I would have done anything to get Mike back.

"Now there are only nineteen working models, and I have all of them."

The technician was still gaping. I could see his tonsils.

"I want to talk to the boss," I said. "Not your supervisor or even his boss. I want to talk to the head honcho, the king of the hill, the man in charge, and I want to talk to him now. I will break another computer every fifteen minutes and another antique every ten minutes. Better hurry."

At my signal, Carl cut the picture on our end. The tech could no longer see us, and he forgot we could see him. He scrambled to find a phone. He used a videophone, but I refused to let myself be distracted. I set my watch and made Jimmy the official timekeeper.

I had to smash a typewriter before the tech got hold of his supervisor, and it took two more computers and a sewing machine to convince her we were serious.

"I'll call the police," she said.

"The whole town is evacuating. The police are busy. They're not real cops anyway, are they? And if you do round up some authentic ones, we'll destroy all the Apples at once."

The supervisor looked worried. The destruction wasn't something she wanted to be responsible for.

The next hurdle was harder.

She brought in Wendy's father, Mr. Lindstrom.

Wendy looked as if she'd been sucker-punched when he came on the screen.

"That's low," I said to Mr. Lindstrom. "Really, really low."

He ignored me, incredulous. "Wendy, what

are you doing there? What's going on? Where did you get all that TV equipment?"

She didn't say anything.

"My God, Wendy, tell me you don't have anything to do with this . . . wanton destruction."

Silence.

He closed his eyes, in pain. "Are you doing this to hurt me? I thought you were happy about the baby."

"I am." Her head was lowered, eyes hidden in her long dark bangs.

"Then why?" It was a cry from the soul. Mr. Lindstrom was an archaeologist, a historian; the destruction of antiques sifted painstakingly from garbage-dump graveyards was akin to murder in his eyes.

Jimmy's watch beeped. "Time," he said.

"Bring out the next computer," I said without lifting my gaze from the screen.

"Angel." He looked disappointed. "This is unworthy of you."

"Lives are more precious than things. You can stop the wanton destruction if you want to." I made my voice gentler than necessary. I liked Mr. Lindstrom. "They're using you to get to me through Wendy. Don't let them do it." I picked up the baseball bat. "I won't deal with anyone but the boss."

"I am the boss."

I hadn't seen that one coming, and I choked on a laugh when I realized he wasn't lying. "Wendy?"

"He's the project manager for the Chinchaga

Historical Immersion Project," she said flatly. "Do you think I would have been admitted otherwise?"

I started breathing again. "He's just a step on the ladder, then. He didn't know about the hidden TV cameras." I hefted the bat and addressed the screen. "Go get the next person up the chain."

Wendy grasped the handle of the bat. I held on to it for a moment, looking into her pain-darkened eyes, then surrendered it.

Relief made a road map of Mr. Lindstrom's face. "You've made the right decision— *No!*"

Wendy held the bat high over the computer like an executioner's sword. She took several preparatory swings, like a batter warming up, while her father pleaded with her to stop.

She didn't seem to hear; she licked her lips, gaze intent and tightly focused, as if in a trance.

Her first blow was tentative, barely jarring the monitor where it sat on the CPU. Her second tipped it off the pedestal and cracked the screen. After her third stroke imploded the cathode-ray tube, she went berserk.

She clubbed the computer as if it had just betrayed her. Tears sheened her eyes. "This is for the time you went off to Peru and left me behind." Thunk. "This is for the kachina doll you brought me back from New Mexico." Crash. Mr. Lindstrom flinched with every swing. "And the pottery shard from Laos. Did you think it made up for your absence?" The monitor lay in splinters on the floor now, the keys scattered like dice, the drive boxes cracked, but she kept bashing and bashing until Carl gently plucked the bat from her hands.

He pressed her face against his shirt and looked over her shoulder at Mr. Lindstrom's image on the monitor. "She doesn't mean it." His voice was flat. "This week has been very traumatic for her."

Mr. Lindstrom went off the deep end. "Don't you tell me about *my* daughter, you computer! How can you understand her feelings when you don't have any of your own?"

Carl didn't react to the insult, just quietly ushered Wendy offscreen.

Jimmy's watch beeped again. I gave him the nod. "Kill a VCR." He did so efficiently, with a minimum of fuss.

The distant crash forced Mr. Lindstrom's head up. "I need to talk to your boss," I told him.

"Cynthia's trying to get him on the tube right now," he said moodily. "He's in Japan, and it's five in the morning there. The connection's going to take some time."

In Japan, when they'd just taken Mike? I don't *think* so. "Better hurry. You have exactly nine minutes before another piece of your history disappears forever."

Mr. Lindstrom spent all nine of them trying to make me feel guilty about the treasures I was destroying.

"What about the treasures of mine you've destroyed?" I countered, but he only looked bewildered. Questions about Project Renaissance would have to wait until Mr. Japan appeared.

Two computers later Mr. Japan came on. He didn't look tired to me: he looked hopping mad. He didn't wait for me to talk, just started ranting about tear gas and punishing us to the full extent of the law.

"Punishment?" I raised an eyebrow. "What are you going to do? You've already kept me in prison for seventeen years of my life."

He didn't seem to hear. I had to dismantle a sewing machine in front of him before he finally shut up. "Are you ready to hear my demands now?" I asked. "They're quite simple; you shouldn't have any problem understanding them."

He glowered at me.

"Yes or no?" I asked sweetly, stripping the casing off a pocket calculator.

"Yes!"

"Good. I want Mike back." I started to give him an ultimatum, but he cut me off.

"Mike who?"

"Oh, come on! You know who. My other half."

"Half of what?"

I was so mad I killed two Apples before his screaming got through.

"I don't know anyone named Mike!" He turned to his executive assistant: "Get me a list! Get me a list! What the hell town is she from?"

"Renaissance," I said.

"Renaissance, Canada?"

I swore. I believed him. "Carl, go back to Mr. Lindstrom." He cut Mr. Japan off midsquawk.

Mr. Lindstrom hadn't moved, his head in his hands.

"Mr. Lindstrom!"

His head came up slowly, face ravaged. Of course, with a new baby he probably hadn't gotten much sleep last night. "Angel?"

"Your boss can't help me. I need someone else, the head of the Renaissance Project."

He looked just as puzzled as Mr. Japan had. Apparently, Renaissance was using the Historical Immersion Project without the project leaders' knowledge. But there had to be a link somewhere.

"Where do you send your reports?" I asked.

"To Mr. Tajamura."

"No." I shook my head. "The special reports. The ones that profile only a few students, like Mike and me. The ones that accused me of cheating on your social studies test."

His face cleared a little. "You mean the reports for special funding?"

"Yes! Those are the ones. I need to contact those people."

Jimmy's watch beeped, and Mr. Lindstrom flinched.

"It's okay," I soothed him. "You have two freebies. This is my fault for following the wrong path. Can you get hold of the grant people?"

"I suppose." He looked doubtful.

"Do it."

It took time. Both freebies ticked away, and we started destroying computers again. We were down to ten now, and everyone was getting a little tired of smashing them.

"Anyone want to take a closer look?" I asked.

Carl rolled up his sleeves. "I've always wanted to take one of these apart."

The dismantling spelled a kind of torture to Mr. Lindstrom. "Don't!" He was reduced to pleading as if Carl were an actual human being.

"I'm not hurting it," Carl said calmly. He unscrewed the back. "It has no eyes to pierce, no heart to cut, no feelings to bruise." He lifted the microchip board out. "It's not alive."

"It's a national treasure!"

Carl looked up, blue-gray eyes steady. "It has no soul. By what right do you compare it to me?"

Mr. Lindstrom shut up.

It occurred to me that Carl was very, very angry, though, as usual, nothing showed in either his voice or his face. "How is it similar to me? Show me how it is the same, and I'll put it back together again."

Mr. Lindstrom's nostrils flared. "You're both just computers, made out of plastic and silicon."

"A fruit fly has chromosomes like you. Are you the same?"

"A fruit fly doesn't pretend to be other than what it is. You're an impostor." Mr. Lindstrom glared.

Wendy opened her mouth to speak, but Carl stopped her with a motion. "No, let me defend myself." He turned back to Mr. Lindstrom.

"I have a mother and a father, just like you. I was born, as you were. My lungs were only half-developed, and my heart was weak, so instead of abandoning me to a half-existence in a bubble, my parents saw to it that I received mechanical

Augmentation. The scientists did nothing to my brain. I am as human as you are."

"You don't laugh, you don't cry, you don't get angry. You have no emotions, no foibles, no capacity for love. How can you call yourself human?"

Wendy bit her lip to keep from speaking.

Carl took the points one at a time. "My voice box is manufactured, like the rest of me. I can laugh, but the sound is unnatural, so I prefer not to. My Augmented body does not produce the hormone that causes human tears, but that doesn't mean I'm never sad. I feel. I love."

Wendy could hold back no longer. She wrapped her arms around Carl's waist like a kudzu vine. "And I love him, so just shut up, Daddy. You're wrong." She kicked the Apple II, and they walked away from the monitors, down to the far end of the attic.

I told Jimmy to take charge of the antiques for a while and faced Mr. Lindstrom, who looked more desperate than ever. "You're going to lose your daughter if you don't stop attacking Carl like that."

He shook his head. "She doesn't really love him. It's a rebellion. She started dating him the day Raven and I told her we were going to have a baby."

"But you had problems with her before the baby."

"For years."

"Let me guess: they started just after you and her mother got divorced, right? Wendy started slipping away, and you don't know why?"

Mr. Lindstrom flushed at the edge in my voice. "Family structures have changed over the years. It was only a contract marriage. Her mother and I had always planned to go our separate ways after Wendy turned five. The digs I went on weren't suitable for children, so Wendy lived with her mother. For a while she would beg me to take her with me. Then one day she stopped asking." He looked away.

"Did you ever stop and think maybe she wanted to go with you because she was being mistreated by her mother or stepfather?" I asked scornfully.

"What?" He looked startled at the idea. "Oh, the eighties bugaboo, abuse. No, it's different in the future. The psychologists have tests. If there's even a possibility of abusiveness, the person wouldn't be allowed to have children, and Noreen and her second husband had a little boy of their own."

The last piece tumbled into place.

"Would you like to get your daughter back?"

"Why do you think we moved here?" he asked bitterly. "It was so we could grow into a family. I think it was actually working, before Raven got pregnant."

"I can help you." Wendy would be furious with me for breaking a confidence, but I wasn't sure if I would ever see her again after today, and I wanted to help my best friend. "I may need support later on. If I help you, will you do me a favor?"

He smiled faintly, unbelieving. "If you can get

me my daughter back, I'll sign my house over to you."

"A favor's all I need," I said easily. I probably wouldn't even need that. It was strictly insurance. "Let's start with Carl. She loves him now, but that wasn't why she started dating him. Do you know why she did?"

"I already told you: because she was mad at me, and she knew I would disapprove."

"Wrong. She did it because you hurt her, and she felt a kinship with Carl."

"Kinship? With a robot?"

"She's tried to tell you a hundred times," I said gently. "She told you every time you asked her why she didn't play the piano anymore. Do you remember what she said? 'Because I have a tin ear.' "

It took him several seconds to comprehend, and then he denied it. "*No*. I saw her when she was born. She was perfect. She's not a robot."

"No, she's not. Neither is Carl. But she does have an artificial ear. I imagine she got it one of those times when you were off on a dig and her stepfather slammed her head into a coffee table."

"No." He kept shaking his head. "Impossible. He wouldn't have been allowed to have children."

"I don't think he did. I think he and Noreen tricked you. I think she deliberately waited until your divorce was nearing and allowed herself to get pregnant. I think Lee was your child and Wendy knew it. When she begged you to take her away, did she beg you to take Lee, too?"

I read the answer in Mr. Lindstrom's bloodless face.

"That's why she's so upset with you about the baby, because she thinks you're replacing Lee, whom she loved but you ignored. And that's why she's so protective of this baby even when it was still in the womb. She failed Lee; she would die before she let harm befall another brother."

Mr. Lindstrom's mouth moved, but no sound came out at first. He wet his lips and tried again. "Lee. He—he died in a boating accident. He was run over by their own speedboat. Wendy—Wendy jumped in and pulled him out. All bruised. The father went to jail for criminal neglect, too much alcohol in his blood. Oh, God—" He started weeping. "You don't think—"

I did think. Lee was probably beaten to death and the accident faked. And Wendy had been carrying that knowledge all this time. She would have been thirteen at the time and helpless.

"My son," Mr. Lindstrom was saying. "Wendy . . ."

"I'll get her," I said gently—

—and the picture fuzzed out, the connection cut. I found myself face-to-face with the screen image of a large, obese man.

No time to call Wendy. I shifted gears abruptly, blinking back my own tears. Lee was four years dead; Mike was missing now. A crack had appeared in the wall of silence surrounding Project Renaissance, and I had to exploit it to the max or lose him. I studied my opponent.

The man had brown hair, sideburns, a large nose, and thick glasses. The smile on his full lips was not matched in warmth by his pale blue eyes.

"Hello, Uncle Albert," I said flatly. "Where's Aunt Patty?"

"I think we've gone beyond such charades," he said. "My name is Dr. Frank."

Not just a spy, then, but one of the scientists. "Dr. Frankenstein." The name came automatically to my lips, bringing with it a flash of memory. Hadn't there been a doctor at the Orphanage whom Nikita had called Dr. Frankenstein? Was this the same one?

"As you wish, Angel." Dr. Frankenstein's voice was surprisingly rich. He had used a somewhat different voice for the role of inept Uncle Albert. "Dare I ask what you're up to now? And where your partner in crime, Mike, is?"

Hope jolted my heart. Had Mike escaped, then?

Dr. Frankenstein was watching me very closely, his full lips pursed.

I bounced back down to earth. "Don't give me that crap. You have Mike, and I want him back."

Dr. Frankenstein blinked, his eyes magnified hugely by his glasses. "An interesting ploy. Are you trying to make me think you don't know where Mike went when he escaped? Hmmm. I shall have to think about this."

The screen went blank.

I didn't turn away. "I know you're still watching me. And your ploy won't work either. Let Mike go or I'll take this town apart brick by brick."

Dr. Frankenstein reappeared. "From what I hear, you've already made a fair start. Shall we deal, then? You stop indulging your criminal tendencies, and I'll take you to Mike."

"Uh-uh." I shook my head. "No dice. I keep killing typewriters until Mike's standing in front of me."

"Who do you think you're dealing with? Your dumb jock of a coach? An archaeologist like your friend's father? I don't care how many artifacts you chop up. Not one of them is as rare as one of the violet-eyed. If you want to see Mike, you have to come to us."

"Now, that really would make me stupid, putting myself in your power."

He looked amused. "You're already in my power."

"Not for long," I said softly.

The smile was wiped from his face like chalk under the sweep of an eraser. "No," he said. "Mr. Tajamura will make the connection between the cameras and funding for the Renaissance Project in a couple of hours at the most. You've destroyed his pet project, and he'll be sure to pull Renaissance down with him. But that will take time. By the time the newshounds arrive Mike will be hidden so deep you'll never see him again. I swear it."

I believed him. My bluff had been called. "You win," I said. *For now.*

"Splendid. An aircar will pick you up in ten minutes." The screen greened out.

CHAPTER

13

I STOOD ALONE on the school lawn as an aircar alighted like a butterfly in front of me. Wendy and the others had wanted to wave me off, but I had insisted they wait out of sight. I didn't want to cause any more trouble for them than I already had.

The back windows of the aircar were tinted black. The rest of the craft was white, a small, sleek plane the length of a station wagon. It had stubby wings, tail fins, and a bullet nose. I could see four engines poking out of the back and sides, but they gave off only a full-throated growl.

I kept my expression blasé, refusing to be impressed by the next century's version of a car.

I'd had vague notions of jumping the pilot and making him take me to Mike, but the pilot stayed safely inside the separate cockpit. The passenger door slid open, and I climbed inside.

A single seat faced backward, overlooking a compact cargo space, and I sat down. I had barely fastened the webbed seat belt when the aircar lifted straight up off the ground. As we accelerated forward, I looked toward the windows to see what direction we were going, but the black tint shut everything out. For all I knew, the pilot might fly a wide, wide circle in the air, then land right back where we had started once it got too dark for me to see.

The idea intrigued me and, partly out of boredom and partly because I didn't want to think about what lay ahead, I ran with it. What buildings in Chinchaga might house the brain cortex of the Renaissance Project?

It would have to be a fairly large building and also one that I would have no reason ever to go inside.

The town hall, the fire station, the hospital, the old folks' home? Not the town hall, because I'd written my driver's license test there. The firehouse would need to be maintained in case of a real emergency. While I'd never been sick for more than a day in my entire life, I had visited Maryanne in the hospital once.

The old folks' home chimed as a possibility. I couldn't remember any of my friends visiting relatives there—which wasn't surprising considering the Historical Immersion scam. Chinchaga was understaffed when it came to children and senior citizens.

I was still going over possibilities when the aircar landed several hours later. Darkness had fallen, and four sober men in gray-and-black military uniforms escorted me the short distance from the aircar to the Renaissance building—four armed men. I felt positively dangerous.

Trees lined the walk, eliminating several locations. The placement of the trees seemed right for Chinchaga's retirement home, but I had paid so little attention to the place that I couldn't be sure.

In daylight the main floor could have been a sunny place to play cards and while away one's golden years. I caught a glimpse of lots of plants and windows before the guards led me down a dimly lit carpeted hall to a series of four doors, each locked and bolted, in the center of the building. I didn't realize the last door opened to an elevator cage until the floor began to sink.

Dr. Frankenstein and Mike were waiting for me when the elevator doors opened. "Welcome home, Angel," Dr. Frankenstein said.

I ignored him and walked straight into Mike's arms.

I surprised Mike a little—his arms hung stiff for a second before coming around me—but I'd already betrayed my feelings so I saw little point in pretending I didn't care for him.

Mike let go of me too soon—I hadn't realized until I touched him again how worried I'd actually been. "Angel, you remember Leona and Vincent Cole, don't you?"

I turned and saw two more people standing in the wings. "Of course." I even smiled, but I didn't like the intense way Leona was looking at me.

"Well, Angel, you've had a very busy day," Dr. Frankenstein said patronizingly. "I'm sure you'll be wanting to go to sleep. Vincent, why don't you show Angel to her room? A tour can wait until tomorrow."

Vincent took my arm, separating me from Mike. I started to jerk free, but Mike gave a little nod. He'd been here longer than I had and must know something. I went with Vincent to the elevator. God, I was tired.

Vincent hit the button for B2—the subbasement, I presumed. A key was required to get back up to the ground floor.

"Have you been here long?" I asked, when it became obvious that Vincent wasn't going to say anything.

"Yes."

I persisted, following him out of the elevator. "How long, exactly?" I was wondering if they'd been here since the badminton tournament, so Vincent's answer stunned me.

"We live here."

I stopped dead in the middle of the hall. The overhead camera swiveled and focused on me. "What? For how long?"

"Since our fourteenth birthday."

"What happened? Did they just come and take you?"

He looked amused. "Hardly. No, we offered them a deal. We would stop pretending to be stupid and start working for them, if they paid us money."

I shook my head sadly. "You poor naive innocents."

A little red color stung Vincent's cheeks. "It was the smartest thing we ever did."

"We? Meaning you and Leona?" I raised an eyebrow.

"We're much better off here than we were in that museum."

"Yes, I can see that." I trailed one hand along the wall tiled in dark green. Two levels down, no sunlight.

I'd succeeded in making Vincent angry and defensive.

"Their funding won't last forever, you know," he warned me. "When it ends, you and your friend will be thrown out into the snow, penniless, barely able to speak the language, unable to do simple things like dial a phone, much less get a job. Leona and I will have a cushion."

His remarks about getting a job and not knowing the technology sounded depressingly real, but I reminded myself that there were always careers in the arts. All you needed to be a dancer, for instance, was a supple body and good coordination, which I had in spades.

"You and Leona *will* have money?" I repeated. "You don't have it yet? Let me guess, the good doctor Frankenstein is holding it in trust for you."

"We have money."

"Oh, and what have you bought with it?" I gestured at the hallway again. "Looks as though there are a lot of shops here."

"We go on field trips," Vincent said through clenched teeth.

I kept poking fun at him. "Oh, wow, you get to see the inside of two malls a year, is that it? They are treating you splendidly. Like a king."

Vincent stopped. "You're to stay in this room. The docs will probably test you tomorrow, so rest up."

"Don't worry," I said. "I have every intention of sleeping in." And no intention of doing any tests.

Vincent seemed to read my mind. "Wait until he makes you an offer you can't refuse, babe. You'll cooperate. Here's your door. There's a puzzle lock on it. You have five minutes to solve it or you sleep standing up in the hallway."

"Cute. Do you pet monkeys do tricks for food, too?"

"At least I'm getting paid to do tricks. Think about it."

"I'd rather be a caged falcon than a tame pigeon," I said to his retreating back.

I thought seriously about exploring the halls or smashing the lock but decided I was too bone-weary to start any battles tonight. The lock consisted of a four-by-four-inch square with fifteen sliding tiles that, when correctly arranged, formed a picture. It took me two minutes.

A grotesquely fat walrus leered at me from the lock panel.

"Very cute." I didn't bother turning on the lights, suspecting that they, too, would have some sort of puzzle. Five minutes later I was sacked out on the bed. Ten minutes later I was asleep.

I woke up when someone put a hand over my mouth.

I was sleeping fully clothed on top of the covers, and I had raised my legs for a brutal kick, when I recognized Mike's voice. "Shhh. It's just me."

"Took you long enough," I grumbled, but inside I felt a warm glow of happiness. Let the scientists do their damnedest, we were together.

Our lips met, but the possibility of infrared cameras kept the kiss fairly short. Likewise, we only asked questions the doctors already knew the answers to.

"How did they take you?" I asked.

"They were waiting for me when I got home." He shrugged. "They were armed, so I didn't argue. Where have you been? I expected you to be in the same aircar I was in. Did you escape?"

"No. I didn't find out you were gone until the next morning when I went jogging." I explained briefly about the cameras, the riot, and all the broken computers.

Mike was silent for a moment. "So why are you here? They wouldn't have dared to touch you in front of so many witnesses."

"Because you're here, silly. Because we're a team." *Because I couldn't bear to lose you*. Then, awkwardly, when Mike didn't respond, "Wouldn't you have come for me?"

He didn't answer, getting up. "I should get back to my room now. Breakfast's at six, and if you're not there they don't feed you."

In hurt silence, I watched him go.

He stopped at the door. "All right, I would have come." His voice was fierce. "But it still would have been a frigging stupid thing to do. You broke open their Historical Immersion scheme. Following me into their clutches just gives them another weapon to use against both of us." He glided out the door.

A small snap told me he'd removed one of the puzzle pieces and mixed up the rest so no one else could get in.

I woke up in a bad mood the next morning, compounded by the discovery that punching in w-a-t-e-r on the shower dial after I broke the code produced only *cold* water. Warm had to be specified.

For breakfast Mike and I were served cold toast with very sour crabapple jelly while Leona and Vincent dined on Belgian waffles with whipped cream and strawberries.

Subtle, Dr. Frankenstein was not. It amused me that food was his weapon of choice. I remembered how once "Uncle Albert" had brought me a huge chocolate bar but refused to give it to me until I recited my multiplication tables. Even in grade three I was too smart to fall for that and began a whining campaign instead until, obviously unused to children, Uncle Albert gave me the chocolate bar. I immediately turned back into my sunny self.

Leona pointedly ignored me all through breakfast. She spoke to Mike, though, flirting. "When the doctors are done with you this afternoon, you have to come up to my room. I've got some cassettes, and you promised to teach me that dance step you showed me at the badminton tournament."

"If I have time," Mike said, but there was a razor edge to his smile that kept me from wishing anything worse on her than acne—and chubbiness.

The only time Leona looked away from Mike was to glare at her silent brother and his half-full plate. "Eat or I'll throw up." She opened her mouth and made as if to stick her finger down her throat. Vincent grimaced but dutifully polished off his waffle.

Mike and I exchanged glances. What was that all about?

A scientist in a white lab coat separated me from the others after breakfast.

"Angel Eastland?" She pumped my hand, quick and energetic. "My name's Catherine Berringer; it's a pleasure to meet you at last." I'd halfway been expecting Aunt Patty, but Catherine was a stranger in her midthirties, blond, attractive, with a blinding smile. I could immediately see why Dr. Frankenstein had chosen her to give the speech. She reeked of sincerity and enthusiasm, interspersing her tour with propaganda.

"This is the game room. We've tried to make the tests as fun and challenging as possible."

The place was a dazzling Disneyland of future wonders. Instead of board games like Monopoly and Clue, there were interactive holographs of murder mysteries, puzzles made out of twisted metal with dozens of possible movements, and war game simulations where you could choose to reenact battles from the time of Alexander the Great up to wars I hadn't even heard of because they hadn't been fought yet in 1987.

My fingers itched to press the buttons, but I forced myself to look unimpressed. "Games stop being fun when they become homework."

Catherine wasn't stupid. She must have sensed my interest, but she only smiled and said, "Well, we have plenty of plain old boring tests for you to take, too."

I felt like an ungrateful wretch, but I couldn't let my liking for Catherine weaken my purpose. "What if I refuse?"

"Obviously we can't force you to take the tests."

That never stopped you before.

"But we're hoping that you will take them. The project doesn't exist to torment you, Angel," she said gently. "We have a purpose, an important one."

"Don't tell me; I don't want to know. I'm sure it's a very good purpose, very noble. But I don't care."

She looked disappointed but not angry. "All right. But you're only postponing the inevitable."

We visited the gym next. Aside from a small track to run laps around, almost all the space was taken up by exercise machines—more technological wonders that measured your heartbeat and

even the amount of fatigue poisons in your muscles. Catherine proudly pointed out the tiny badminton court and rackets. "You and Mike may
continue practicing every day if you'd like. We'll
even bring in your coach. Rick Hrudey was considered the best un-Augmented badminton player
in the world in his time."

The goody she was offering me lacked spice. I
liked playing badminton because I liked exercis-
ing. The Olympic dream had only been a means
to an end.

I put out another feeler. "Did Coach Hrudey
surprise you when he offered to coach Mike and
me to stardom?"

"Oh, yes," Catherine admitted readily.
"Everyone knew, of course, that he was searching
for an un-Augmented team to train. He's been
very vocal about his quest to bring back the pres-
tige of the old Olympics, touting a contest of muscle and skill instead of machine against machine.
Since modern schools don't promote competitive
sports, he turned to the Historical Immersion
Project. But we were shocked when he picked
you. Prior to that, popular wisdom ran that your
fondness for sports was just an effort to overcom-
pensate for the mental skills you were repressing.
It was Dr. Frank who finally theorized that the
Renaissance genes produced physical as well as
mental superiority."

I hadn't been overcompensating, but she was
partly right: sports and drama and social events
had been safe ways to show my personality.

"So where's Dave?" I asked.

"Who?" She looked puzzled.

"Dave. You know," I said sarcastically, "the sportswear rep."

Her face remained uncomprehending.

"Dave the Terrorist." I tried again. "The radical who kidnapped Mike and me."

"He's in jail, I imagine," Catherine said, powder blue eyes wide. I studied her closely, but as far as I could tell she wasn't evading my question. She really didn't know Dave was on the scientists' side. "I saw him get arrested on the news. You're not afraid of him, are you? The Institute is very secure," she assured me.

"Ah, but is it secure from the outside or only from the inside?"

Catherine blinked, then forged ahead with her speech. Terrorists didn't interest her. "You and Mike have incredible gifts—intellect, athletic ability, leadership—and we've only scratched the surface. Both of you embody the true Renaissance ideal: the rebirth of humankind. You have so much to share." Her eyes shone with zeal.

I punctured her balloon rudely. "What makes you think we're willing to share? If you wanted our help, you shouldn't have treated us like prisoners."

A hit.

Her hands fluttered in distress. "They were wrong to put you in the Orphanage when you were just babies. I've always disagreed with that. But you have to realize that the discovery of a new subspecies of human sent a shock wave through the world.

"For months afterward the media were full of wild speculations on the origin of the Renaissance children: aliens impregnating human women, evil genetic experiments dating back to the Cold War, descendants of ancient Atlanteans. All sorts of baloney."

"And what was the truth?" My heart was beating harder than it should have been. I was who I was; my beginnings shouldn't have mattered to me, but they did.

"That you were the top secret project of President Needham's North American government. Genetic engineering was performed on fifty of you at the one-cell stage. We don't know much more than that. When you were discovered, a lot of computer databases were wiped clean."

"Exactly how were we discovered, anyway?"

"Purely by accident. A reporter was digging for some dirt on an entirely different issue and stumbled across a few references to Project Renaissance. He blew the whistle, and a United Nations watchdog team was sent in. The whole house of cards that the Needham government had built came tumbling down when the team discovered fifty violet-eyed babies. Babies who were genetically different."

"What kind of differences?" I knew I was smarter than most people were, but intelligence shouldn't show up in one's DNA.

"Your brains are more complex. Almost without exception Renaissance children are born without appendixes and never develop wisdom teeth. Your immune systems work faster, your reflexes are astonishing, your bodies produce different hormones, your menstrual cycle is not the same. . . . I could go on for hours. Small things, but recognizable and always an improvement. The media started to call you the Inheritors of the Earth." She paused. "Would you like to see a clipping file?"

I nodded and followed her to her office. I paged through the file slowly. A toddler with violet eyes on the cover of *Time*. Hysterical letters to the editor, calling for our extermination. "Noted Scientist Says Renaissance Children Should Be Sterilized." I looked at that one a long time.

"Many people saw you as a threat to their children's future," Catherine said quietly. "An elite who would gobble up all the wealth and good jobs and take over the government. There were riots over the issue."

Another picture of people bashing each other over the head with signs that said Devil-Spawn and Inheritors.

"The government of the time institutionalized you partly for your own protection," Catherine said.

"How altruistic," I said sarcastically.

She hurried on under my glare. "They had tunnel vision, of course. They couldn't see beyond the immediate public-relations problem. But the current project head holds very different views. Why, the first thing Dr. Frank did when he got promoted was place all of you in loving homes."

Loving? I had lucked out, but what about Mike? And Leona and Vincent hadn't shown much hesitation about bailing out of their supposedly perfect family.

I shook my head. "You've done a lot more than just tear us from our homes. You've violated every aspect of my life, of my privacy. Curtailed every freedom. I don't owe you a thing."

She didn't have a comeback for that, and we resumed the tour in silence. The next stop was the test room. "This is Dr. Boleyn. He keeps statistics and compiles the test results. Would you like to hear your scores?"

"No thanks." I already knew my scores. "I have an average of fifty-one percent in my academic courses. I took great care to maintain it."

Dr. Boleyn was a graybeard. When he shook his head his long beard swung back and forth like a pendulum. "Not quite, Miss Eastland. We realized, of course, what you were doing right away. Sometimes you got every second question wrong as a way of taunting us. Or every first, second, fourth, seventh and eleventh wrong, making a pattern. Getting exactly fifty percent every time is just as revealing as getting one hundred percent."

His pompous smirk made me ache to punch him. "But not revealing enough," I said. "You could prove we were smart, but not that we were geniuses, or you would have pulled us out of the Historical Immersion Project sooner."

I marched out of the room, and Catherine

had to break into a fast trot. She made no comment, still cheerful.

"And this office belongs to Dr. Estevez. She's our resident psychologist. Feel free to drop by any time and have a chat with her if you're feeling frustrated or unhappy."

I just looked at her. "If you want to raise prisoners' morale, you have to set them free first."

My words flew in one ear and out the other. She looked more determined than ever. "This doesn't have to be a jail, Angel. Just think. You were a child when you made the decision to hide your gift. *You can change your mind.*" She said this as if it were a great revelation. "There are issues at stake that you were too young to understand. It has been my opinion all along that you should have been told at age thirteen or fourteen and allowed to make a decision based on the true facts."

"Which are?"

She became very serious. "Toxic wastes, pollution, and the breakdown of the ozone layer have weakened the human race. In each generation more and more children are born with serious birth defects, one in ten of which is correctable only by Augmentation. The incidence is even higher among the Spacers. Human genes are becoming very fragile. People get sick more often and for longer. You, Mike, Vincent, and Leona have spent only one day in the hospital among the four of you, and that was for a concussion. The tinkering that was done to your genes is against the law, but now that you're here, you're needed. We need your DNA to strengthen the human race, and we need you to become scientists and help to cure us."

It sounded good: the saviors of the human race. I imagined the politicians would have rallied to their cry.

But I had no desire to be a savior. It wasn't that I wanted to rob banks; I just wanted to make my own choices.

"What a load of BS. You don't need a cure. You've already found one: Augmentation. Carl is no less a human being than someone wearing glasses to counteract myopia. It's your own prejudice that's making you grasp at straws."

Sadness clouded her face. "You don't understand. Soon we'll all be Augmented."

"So?"

She just kept talking. "You have a gift." Blah, blah, blah. "You have a responsibility." The ultimate guilt trip. She couldn't understand my refusal. "We're offering you a career, training, anything you want."

"Sorry. I don't think lab rats have much of a job future."

I was almost looking forward to seeing Dr. Frankenstein again at the end of the tour. At least he didn't believe his own lies.

It was lunchtime before Catherine finished exhaustively detailing the facilities. I ditched her and headed for the cafeteria. Mike and Leona were already eating. Their heads were close together; they were in the middle of an intense conversation that rang warning bells with me.

"You didn't fall for her lies again, did you?" Leona was asking.

"No," Mike said. "How could I? I've already fallen for you, Leona."

My heart gave a terrible lurch.

"You're so pure. Your eyes are like amethysts," Mike said. "And your lips . . . your lips drip venom."

"My God," Leona said, "you *do* believe her."

I resumed walking, my panic easing. I didn't know what was going on between Mike and Leona, but I would find out.

They were sitting at a two-person table while Vincent sat alone at the next table. The polite thing to do would have been to sit with him.

I've never had much of a problem being rude. I pulled up a chair and plunked my ham sandwich and myself down between Mike and Leona. "Hi there," I said cheerily.

Mike's shoulders stiffened, then relaxed. "Hi yourself." He looked amused at my blatant staking-out of territory. I didn't care.

"Be careful, you'll knock over my drink." Leona looked annoyed.

"Hmm, there isn't much room, is there?" I said, as if just noticing this. "Let's push the two tables together."

We did this, and Vincent's sparkling wit joined the lively discussion. Not.

Me: "So, Vincent, what's on the schedule for this afternoon?"

Vincent: "Depends."

Me: "On what?"

Vincent: "Lots of things."

I rolled my eyes at Mike. He winked back. "Well, in that case we might as well finish our championship game," I said.

"It's already over," Leona said quickly. "You forfeited when you ran off the court."

"Ha. As I recall, you were scrambling to return one of my shots. I didn't hear your racket twang into it when the lights went out," I lied. "You missed; we won."

The ensuing argument lasted longer than my ham sandwich and was still raging when we reached the court. While we were warming up, a technician came for Mike. "They need you in Dr. Estevez's office."

"And if I refuse to go?" Mike inquired.

The techie didn't back down. "I'll call the guards and they'll tow you there."

"Call away." Mike served the birdie.

It was no bluff. Mike didn't resist, but he didn't help, either. Two large guards dragged away his limp body, like a passive resistance protester at a peace rally.

I turned to Leona. "Singles?"

She nodded. She and Vincent exchanged a brief glance, and he left the room like an obedient dog.

We played one set to five—fast, furious, and silent.

Leona broke the silence first. "I want you to leave him alone." She drove a shot past me.

I caught the shuttlecock with the very tip of my racket, bouncing it just over the net. "Do you always get what you want?"

"I do when it concerns Vincent."

She surprised me, and the birdie dropped through a hole in my guard. I had presumed we were talking about Mike. Interesting. "What does Vincent have to say about that?" I served a high clear to the back of the court.

"He leaves things like that to me." The birdie arced back toward me.

"Things like money, too? Are you the one who persuaded him to sell out?" I smashed the white shuttlecock back into her court.

The birdie got caught in her badly strung racket, and I saw real hatred in her expression. "Don't look so damn smug. Once Frankenstein gets his blackmail claws into you, you'll comfort yourself that at least you're getting paid, too." She threw her racket at the wall and stalked out.

I chased after her on impulse. "Wait!"

Her face could have been a stone carving of a faerie, highborn and cruel.

"How is he blackmailing you? Maybe I can help you."

Her eyes scorned the very idea, and she started walking again.

"What can it hurt?"

She stopped. Turned. "You want to help? Somewhere in Dr. Frankenstein's secret files is the location of Vincent's baby. Find it and we'll help you escape."

"Baby?" I couldn't help it; my jaw dropped.

"The history Vincent and I were immersed into wasn't as recent as yours. We got World War II London during the blitz," Leona spoke rapidly, as if fearing interruption. "Vincent fell in love with a girl. Erin Reinders. He got her pregnant. Erin was sent away to the country to have the baby, and he was supposedly given up for adoption, but Frankenstein has him.

"Frankenstein gave us a choice; cooperate or never see the child again. We chose to cooperate." She paused. "That was four months ago. Ever since then Vincent's been depressed. He wants to sleep all day, and if I don't hound him and threaten to become bulimic, he doesn't eat. I'd just finally convinced him things weren't so bleeding bad when you came up with that tame pigeon crap."

I stood in the middle of the room, thinking, for a long time after she'd left. For all her anger, her story sounded genuine to me.

Damn Dr. Frankenstein to hell. I wondered if he had arranged for the girl to get pregnant. Talk about Machiavellian.

Mike returned from the shrink, but my appointment was next, so I got dragged off and didn't get a chance to tell him about Leona's little revelation or to ask him what poison Leona had dripped into his ears.

Dr. Estevez was a brown-skinned woman in her forties with a beautiful soft contralto voice. I recognized her vaguely as having been the school counselor one town back. "I have some

questions I'd like to ask you. We run a psycho-
logical profile of all the residents here. None of
the questions are ones that I would hesitate to
answer myself."

"Bully for you."

"Will you answer my questions, Angel?"

"Ask all you like." I crossed my legs casually
to demonstrate how relaxed I was. "I just don't
promise to tell the truth."

"I often find the lies people choose to tell
more revealing than the truth," Dr. Estevez said.
"Let's start with the basics." She asked me a
series of questions about my family background, all information she already knew.

I alternated between the truth and lies on a
whim, enjoying the subtle battle of wits. The
interview was almost at an end before I realized
Dr. Estevez hated me.

I was accustomed to charming people, and
her carefully hidden dislike made me curious.
"Why don't you like me?"

She didn't prevaricate or insist that she did
like me. "You're very full of self-pity. You keep
harping on the prison that you grew up in, as if
it were some terrible place. Nobody beat you,
you had an excellent education provided free of
charge—"

"I'd hardly call an education a hundred years
out of date excellent."

She continued, unperturbed. "You come from
an unbroken home, went to parties, had many
friends"—one friend, I thought, many acquain-
tances—"have spent the last ten years having a

rousing good time at the taxpayers' expense, but when they ask something of you in return, you spurn them. You have no idea how good you've had it."

"Why don't you tell me?" I suggested. I was pretty sure she would anyhow.

My flippancy annoyed her further. "I will. I was born in a Tenth World country in Central America, a banana republic too poor to feed its own people. The United Nations couldn't maintain the peace there. My parents were shot to death in front of my eyes when I was five. Don't you *dare* tell me how tough you've had it." She flipped her notebook shut and stood, forcing me to leave.

I considered her words carefully, then decided that atrocities committed in another country didn't excuse crimes committed here.

I was thinking so hard that I bumped into a technician in the hallway. His pile of papers slid to the floor. I bent over to help him pick them up on the off chance that I might glimpse something interesting. I shuffled papers—graphs, tests, more graphs—then handed them back to him with a friendly smile. "Here you go. Sorry about that."

My smile listed badly when he clumsily slipped me a folded note.

I was fresh out of pencil cases so I read it right there in the hall—aloud. " 'I can help you find your own kind.' "

I ripped the note into four pieces and scattered them on the floor in front of the techie. He was youngish and thin with intense eyes.

"What do you think I am? Stupid?" I shoved him.

He blinked in owlish alarm, scuttling backward. "What are you talking about?" Blink.

"Nice," I said. "You can tell Dr. Frankenstein you gave it the good old college try, but you failed."

"Dr. Frank? You think I—" Words failed him.

"Duh." I walked away, perversely insulted by the ploy.

My own kind.

Maybe I didn't want to find my own kind. Maybe I happened to like my parents and Wendy and Carl.

CHAPTER

14

MIKE AND I DINED with the charming Dr. Frankenstein that night on French bread, cheddar soup, steak, baby carrots, whipped potatoes, Caesar salad, and a side dish of escargot. The good doctor did like his feed. He chowed down with an enthusiasm that dulled my own appetite.

It occurred to me for the first time that perhaps my mother had purposely burned the chicken Kiev that Uncle Albert had so hated.

"Do I disgust you?" Dr. Frankenstein asked between chews. He popped another whole snail into his mouth, then used a bit of bread to soak up the garlic butter sauce. His sideburns were already shiny with it.

I saw no reason to lie. "Yes."

"Good." He chugged back an entire glass of milk, then smiled coldly. "Thin people tend to underestimate fat people. They associate physical bulk with mental slowness. They're wrong."

He stuffed down another slice of French bread, chewed, swallowed, and smacked his thick lips. "Did you ever wonder why you've met so few fat people?"

"Exercise and smart lifestyle choices?" Mike suggested, his lip curled in disgust.

"Oat bran, you mean?" Dr. Frankenstein chuckled dryly. "Don't be naive. Liposuction. They had it even back in the 1980s. Only in the future it's become much cheaper and more thorough. In addition to vacuuming fat out of your thighs, they can clean the fat deposits out of your arteries. People are just as piggish in the twenty-first century as they were in the twentieth. They are fat people wearing thin bodies, but they are still fat. I choose not to hide my true nature. I am what you see: a glutton."

I cut my T-bone steak into neat bite-size pieces. "You like looking unattractive?"

"As I said, I find it useful to be underestimated. If I were to tell you this room is absolutely free of surveillance cameras and listening devices you wouldn't believe me, would you? 'He's trying to trick us,' you'd think."

"And now you're trying to fast-talk us," Mike said.

"On the contrary. You have it backward. I don't want to trick you into anything. I don't need to: you're already in my hands." He let us savor that particular bit of unpalatable truth while he poured a small lake of gravy onto his plate. Some of it slopped over onto the table-cloth, and a few seconds later he dragged the sleeve of his white suit through it.

"We're not being taped," he continued, "because I don't want what *I* have to say being recorded for posterity." He shoveled in a mouthful of potatoes, talking through the spuds. "So you see, both your assumptions are wrong. I do not always lie, and I care about my own neck more than I care about you."

I affected a look of boredom. "The more you protest your innocence, the less I believe you."

"As you wish." He smiled, showing a sprig of parsley caught between his two front teeth. "I was certainly listening to both of you earlier today. To answer your question, Angel, Dave Belcourt is in jail, and he *was* working for me. He just didn't know it."

I remembered Dave saying, "He'll get you. He's smarter than both of you put together."

Dr. Frankenstein shook his head sadly for the poor deluded fool. "I infiltrated the radicals' circle some time ago. I passed them the information that the favorites in Rick Hrudey's much-publicized badminton demonstration were Renaissance impostors. They wanted to assassinate you, but I persuaded them to torture the location of the rest of your comrades out of you first. They were quite happy to shoot several bullets into the crowd to cause confusion. 'There are some casualties in every war,' Dave said. The terrorist version of 'You can't make an omelette without breaking some eggs,' I suppose. They certainly scrambled a few. Two gun-shot wounds and five people crushed in the stampede."

I stared, unable to say a word in the face of such casual evil.

"My contribution to the scheme was the van, so planting the bugs was easy. You ended the game a little sooner than I had intended, but you proved a theory of mine. Real danger made you show your true colors at last. Too bad it wasn't the kind of evidence I could give to the big boys who hold the purse strings. Silly sheep that they are, it would still occur to them to wonder how the van happened to be bugged."

"What about the Orphanage fire? Was that you, too?" Mike asked.

"Alas, I cannot claim responsibility for that one. The fire was set by some radicals, who have since been jailed. I lost a considerable invest-ment that day. Fortunately, it wasn't a total write-off, as my supervisor kindly got himself asphyxiated.

"The new project head listened to my idea to immerse the remaining dozen Renaissance chil-dren in history. You should have forgotten the need to play dumb within two or three years, lulled by the peace of your new family, and begun manifesting your intelligence again, but you always were contrary, weren't you? Eight children escaped from their incompetent keep-ers, leaving the da Vincis and you and Michael. Seeming duds, all four of you. I got a lot of egg on my face over your lack of results."

I broke into his self-pity, one of his earlier statements bothering me. "If you couldn't use the evidence Dave gained you to trap us, why did you bother doing it?" I asked.

"To prove that he's smarter than we are," Mike said, cold dislike on his face. "Only the game didn't go quite as far as you would have liked, did it, Dr. Frankenstein? You didn't get to ride to the rescue. We jumped Dave all on our own."

"An assumption totally without facts." Dr. Frankenstein's genial smile left his face. He seemed to put it on and take it off like a mask, feeling little genuine amusement. "But then, that seems to be your failing."

"Yours seems to be taking forever to come to the point," I said. "You didn't invite us to dinner for this."

"Don't be impatient. Dinner's not over yet."

I spread my napkin over my steak. "I'm full."

Mike stood up. "Let's go, Angel. He has nothing to say that we need to hear."

"Michael is lying; he doesn't want you to hear what I have to say," Dr. Frankenstein said to me. "He's afraid of what I might tell you about him. I really think you should stay for dessert." For an obese man he moved lightly, taking only seconds to push back his chair and move to the fridge in the corner. With the air of a magician conjuring up rabbits, he produced three glass dishes on a silver tray.

"Strawberry ice cream." He smiled hatefully. "Your favorite, I believe."

CHAPTER

15

MY FIRST THOUGHT was that their listening devices must have been very powerful to have heard us talking over the engine of the bus. I opened my mouth to laugh off Dr. Frankenstein's clumsy attempt to drive a wedge between Mike and me— and then I saw Mike's face, and my vocal cords seized up like a rusty motor.

Mike looked angry—and guilty.

"Do have some ice cream," Dr. Frankenstein said. "It's delicious." He ate a spoonful, smacking his lips and grinning like an evil gnome. I felt a powerful urge to punch my fists into his soft gut until he doubled over and puked.

"We had lemon sherbet last night, didn't we, Mike? We had a nice long conversation and a late night snack when you came in. We shared secrets."

"Don't listen to him. He's lying," Mike said. I read guilt in his desperation. He would have laughed if the accusation hadn't been true.

The freezer hadn't been turned up high enough. The ice cream had melted to a thick sludge, just the way I'd liked it as a child.

"He betrayed you," Dr. Frankenstein murmured in the distant background. "Get back at him. Tell me the secret he shared in return. Nothing important, just a little tiny secret. He told me yours."

But Mike hadn't told me his secret. He hadn't trusted me enough to bare his soul. After the Orphanage fire, he'd chosen unlikable parents so he couldn't be hurt again, and he'd never learned how to let his guard down. But knowing the reason didn't ease the knife in my heart.

"Just one little thing," Dr. Frankenstein said. "One teeny, tiny little thing."

Mike hadn't told me, but I'd guessed enough of his secrets to wound him if I wanted to. He was afraid of heights. He could tolerate them, had climbed down the bridge with me, but he hadn't flipped over the rail. He'd hesitated and stepped over. Mike never hesitated.

"I was trying to gain his trust," Mike said quickly, words running together. "I didn't know you were coming, and I wanted to escape."

I tested the sentence for truth. I wanted to believe it so badly.

"He could have told me chocolate ice cream," Dr. Frankenstein said.

"I did!" Mike said fiercely. "But he was the one who drugged you, and he remembered that it was strawberry."

"He knew I would know," Dr. Frankenstein

said. "He still betrayed you. He said yours was a partnership of convenience only."

Chest aching, I looked down at my bowl of bright pink soup, then up again. "No. Trust has to begin somewhere." I left the room.

The farther out the door I got, the faster my steps became. I jerked at the doorknob to my room and the door popped open, thanks to the plastic card I'd jimmied in it earlier.

I'd covered up all the cameras I could find that morning, but I still went into the shower fully clothed. I raised my face to the jets above, letting the water pummel me. I waited until the air was thick with steam before I allowed myself to cry.

I'd cried millions of fake tears over the years, could dredge up a sniffle at the drop of a hat, but I'd hidden my real tears. I would rather have been caught naked than crying. I leaned against the tile wall and let myself go. I was having a bad week. They'd surprised some tears out of me with the tumble down the stairs, too. Damned if I'd let Dr. Frankenstein know how much his little scheme had hurt me.

He was trying to divide Mike and me. I knew it, but it still hurt. Mike had given him the information so easily, the very first night, only hours after we'd kissed on the bus.

You expect too much of those you love. You always have, I told myself. It didn't help.

I hung my head and let the water fall in torrents.

I was still in the shower when Mike pounded on the door. I knew it was him, but I didn't reply to his calls.

I still hadn't moved when he burst into the bathroom and jerked open the shower door. He came to a full stop when he saw me, dripping wet and still fully dressed. Maybe he'd expected me to cut my wrists in the shower.

He stepped under the water with me and slammed the shower door closed. Within seconds the torrent of water had darkened his hair and plastered his maroon shirt to him. He looked bewildered and angry and so handsome I could hardly bear to look at him. "I thought you were a spy!" he shouted.

"So what changed your mind?" I threw back at him. "Maybe I am a spy."

"I don't know why you're so angry," Mike continued. Water glazed his features, drowned his angry voice. "You thought the same thing about me the night of Maryanne's party. Remember? 'If you're on the scientists' side, I'll carve your heart out with a dull knife,' you said."

"Ah, but you weren't just thinking it. You'd already made up your mind. You proposed that I double-cross them. God, I thought you were joking!"

"So I was just supposed to trust you? Instantly? Like that?" He tried to snap his fingers, but they were too wet.

"Yes! Like that. I trusted *you*."

"I told him what kind of ice cream you once liked. Is that a capital crime?"

"It was a betrayal and you know it." I closed my eyes. "Why are you even here? You still don't trust me."

"Don't be stupid. I know you're not a spy now; I'm not an idiot. I trust you now."

"Do you?" I turned on him like a vampire descending. "Prove it. Tell me something. Tell me a secret."

Mike was silent. The shower beat down on both of us.

"Can't do it? Well, I'll tell it for you, then." I leaned forward and whispered it in his ear. "There, you see? I could have told Dr. Frankenstein, but I didn't. And do you know why?"

"Because you trust me?" Mike said sarcastically.

I hit his shoulder with my palm. "Because I love you. Because I'd rather cut out my tongue than hurt you. *You jerk*. I can't believe I just spent fifteen minutes crying over you." I turned my face to the wall and would not look at him.

After a moment Mike put his arms around me. I stiffened but didn't try to break free.

"I'm sorry, Angel," he murmured near my ear. "You're right. I shouldn't have doubted you."

"No, you shouldn't have. Why did you?"

"Have you ever wanted something so much that you didn't believe it when you finally got it?" Mike asked softly. He looked at the tile walls instead of at me. "They started on me as soon as I got here. I demanded to know where you were, and Dr. Frankenstein said that you were perfectly safe." He paused. "He said it in such a way that I could hear the smirk in his voice, in such a way that he knew I would get upset and insist on seeing you. So he showed me a videotape of you." Another pause.

I was beginning to get the gist of things. "What was I doing?"

"You were dancing. In some kind of 1920s

blues bar. You were wearing a flapper dress, and your hair was different, but it was you."

I had been sound asleep in my own bedroom last night, but I did not doubt Mike. It had likely been old videotape of me, modified and spliced, but still me.

"You were dancing with somebody else. He had violet eyes. Dr. Frankenstein said you had already started your new assignment."

Implying that bringing Mike in had been my last assignment, one that had ended when Mike displayed his cleverness to Dave.

"And you believed him," I said flatly. I didn't care how dazzling the special effects had been; Mike still shouldn't have believed Dr. Frankenstein, our sworn enemy.

Mike shook his head. "My instinctive response was that it wasn't true, but Dr. Frankenstein just kept smiling and shaking his head. He said someday you were going to win an Academy Award for acting."

"And that made you believe him."

Mike's anger began to return; he shook me by the shoulders. "I didn't want to believe him! Don't you understand? I wanted so badly to believe you were innocent that I knew you couldn't be!"

I remembered wading in the river. "Do I terrify you half as much as you terrify me?" Mike had asked, and I had said, "More," because trust was a scary thing. Because if I had trusted and had my trust violated, it would have taken me years to recover from the blow.

"Even then I wasn't sure," Mike went on, "but when Leona showed me my room she said she

had tried to warn me about you at the badminton tournament, that you were Erin
Reinders and had also reeled in Vincent." Mike's
face twisted with bitterness. "That was when I
started to believe Dr. Frankenstein. So when he
asked me for your secret, I told him."

I thought about settling a small score with
Leona the next time I saw her, but that would have
been taking the wrong tack. Dr. Frankenstein had
put her up to it, blackmailed her if she was to be
believed—something I no longer blindly did.

"When you suddenly arrived, I didn't know what
to think. Dr. Frankenstein said, 'Welcome home,' and
I wanted to kill you. I was vibrating with the need.
Then you hugged me, and I knew that Dr.
Frankenstein had lied, that you had never been in his
pay, and that I had betrayed you. That's why I was
angry with you for coming after me, because it meant
I was the one who had betrayed you and I knew Dr.
Frankenstein would tell you sooner or later."

"Which he did, sooner rather than later," I said
wryly. Mike had been manipulated by a master.
"Okay, I forgive you. But if you lose faith in me
again I'll get out that dull knife. Understand?"

"Understood." Mike hesitated, then shared a
secret. "The reason I'm afraid of heights is
because I had to jump from the second floor of
the Orphanage to escape the fire. I still remember the sensation of falling—how it felt like
flying—until I hit the ground. I broke both legs."

I kissed him once, hard, on the lips, then said
gruffly, "Okay, enough soul-searching. Let's blow
this joint. The water's getting cold."

CHAPTER

16

WE SMASHED ALL THE CAMERAS save one. We left that one filming the doorway but turned off the audio. Thus assured that we wanted only privacy, the guards let us alone, ignoring the sounds of destruction from within.

"I'm going to turn this place into kindling!" I yelled banging a lamp against the table edge, while offscreen, Mike began the serious business of battering a hole in the wall.

Medieval man battered down thick castle gates with logs. Thin gypsum board didn't stand much of a chance.

Mike first punched a hole through the gypsum board with a chair leg, then, when that proved awkward because the hole needed to be low to the ground, he lay on his back and hammered at the frail wood with his heels. Cracks appeared and chunks of wall fell to the floor, raising dust.

Since it was an inner wall, there was no insulation. I cleared away the fallen scraps and stored them in the bottom desk drawers, careful to leave no telltale speck. I took a turn on my back, kicking through the wall on the other side while Mike unscrewed half of the lightbulbs and threw them at an invisible bull's-eye on the door as if competing for a carnival prize.

When we finished, the ragged hole was just big enough to wriggle through. On the other side lay a similar but unoccupied bedroom suite.

I grinned at Mike. "Looks nice."

"I'm thinking about making it my life's motto," Mike whispered back. "If the door's locked . . ."

"Go through the wall."

Only the final touches remained. I wrote a note for Dr. Frankenstein and pinned it to the bed. "Don't try to catch us. Where we're going, you can't follow."

It was the literal truth. No way could Dr. Frankenstein fit through that hole, not even after liposuction.

I blew a kiss at the camera and mouthed, "Good-bye," just to speed things up.

Offscreen, we crawled through the hole and, with a lot of grunting effort, pulled the desk back in front of it.

The room was dark, but the layout was identical to that of my room. We pulled this room's desk in front of the hole in the wall, then crawled under the bed and waited. There was a small possibility that the room's cameras were on, recording us, but with so many other locations to watch, I didn't think they would bother with this one.

About ten minutes later we were proved right when a guard knocked on my bedroom door. He spoke in odd, broken cadences, leaving out half his words. "Sorry to disturb, need to confirm you're still there."

"We're not here," Mike sang softly in my ear.

I choked back a giggle.

"Respectfully request to talk," the guard said. "If won't talk will come in."

He didn't sound very enthusiastic. I wondered if he just didn't want to interrupt something embarrassing or if he was worried about getting bonked over the head. He should have been. I'd considered it very seriously.

"Damn hell."

At least the swearwords hadn't changed in a hundred years. I wondered if the guard's strange clipped English was just military jargon or how regular people now spoke. Catherine and the other doctors didn't leave out the pronouns and articles, but that might just have been Historical Immersion training. The thought depressed me.

The guard fumbled with the door, then buzzed some kind of electronic lock. I imagined his eyes widening as he stepped inside and saw the wreckage, then widening further when he realized we weren't there.

I was grinning so hard my cheeks hurt. I'd always adored locked-room mysteries.

"Captain, send backup. Nobody here. Will check bathroom but have bad feeling." I pictured the guard talking into his watch or pen, like James Bond with his spy toys.

Backup arrived. We heard cabinets and closets being opened and air vents poked into, but nobody thought to look behind the desk and nobody saw the plywood in the bottom drawers.

"Progress?" a new voice asked. I decided he was the captain.

"No persons. Just note."

The captain swore. "Better go wake Napoleon."

I convulsed with laughter. Mike stroked my back soothingly. Napoleon was an even better nickname for Dr. Frankenstein—a short little man with a God complex.

It took Dr. Frankenstein another few minutes to arrive.

The captain summarized things for him. "Camera's still filming door. Have to be here somewhere."

" 'Where we're going, you can't follow,' " Dr. Frankenstein quoted, and my guts clenched. Had we been too obvious? "You're assuming," he told the captain. "I could fool the cameras and escape from here if I really wanted to, and so can they."

My heart beat even faster.

"They'll be out in the town by now," Dr. Frankenstein said crisply. "Alert the checkpoints. Start a house-by-house search. Check everywhere—especially small hiding places. The

Renaissance kids are good at making friends. Someone may be hiding them."

"Confining to town won't be easy," the captain said evenly. "Half town has evacuated. Other half is packing up to leave. Riot put hell of scare on everybody."

"Then you'd better try very, very hard." Dr. Frankenstein's voice was soft with menace. I was surprised at how easily the deep, smooth tones carried through the wall.

"Right on it."

The worst danger had passed, but the captain was too thorough—and too sure of the truth his cameras had recorded—not to search the compound. Mike and I had to hide in the bathroom cupboards twice, but the soldiers that came looking expected to find nothing and so did. They rarely did more than look under the bed and check the closet.

Catherine came the closest, mostly by accident.

Dr. Frankenstein's voice from the other side of the wall sent us sliding under the bed. "As you can see, Catherine, they totally destroyed the room. That, coupled with the dead guard and the missing aircar, means we have to consider them potentially violent. I told the guards not to use force unless it was absolutely necessary, but with their comrade dead, I fear they may be a little . . . enthusiastic."

Dead guard? Missing aircar? The fun of putting one over Dr. Frankenstein suddenly vanished like air sucked into a vacuum.

"We don't know that Mike and Angel hurt anyone," Catherine protested. "The military were called in because of rioting all over Chinchaga. Absolutely nothing points to Angel and Mike being responsible. And even if they were, we don't know the circumstances: it could have been self-defense."

Mike and I exchanged glances. We hadn't killed anybody, so who had? Rioters? Dr. Frankenstein, to justify classifying Mike and me as violent? It seemed a little extreme. Then I made the connection. "Leona?" I mouthed the name, and Mike nodded. Leona and Vincent must have taken advantage of the confusion to escape.

I wished them luck, even while feeling chilled. They had killed to get away. How far would Mike and I go to obtain freedom?

"I agree with you entirely," Dr. Frankenstein said soothingly. "But don't you see that from their point of view almost everything will be self-defense? They're a hundred years out of date, remember? Picture a Victorian lady suddenly transported from a small country lane to the five-lane highways so popular in the late twentieth century. She would be startled and terrified, would probably get herself killed. It's the same with these kids. We have no idea what might alarm them or what commonplace little thing might prove fatal. We have to act fast. Mike and Angel must be apprehended before they reach a city. For their own sake as well as others'."

"I suppose you're right." Catherine didn't sound happy about it. Wood creaked, and I realized with a speeding heart that she was leaning against the desk we'd used to hide the hole in the wall. The desk whose drawers were stuffed with give-away chipboard.

"I'd like you to fly out this afternoon," Dr. Frankenstein said. "Coordinate the search from Peace River. With an aircar at their disposal they could go almost anywhere."

"But what about you?" Catherine sounded troubled. Wood creaked again as she got off the desk. I prayed that her slacks wouldn't snag on a partly open drawer. "Shouldn't you be coordinating the search?"

"No, I'm going to stay here and tidy up a few loose ends," Dr. Frankenstein said.

Warning bells sounded in my head. Mike and I exchanged glances. Were we the loose ends? Had Dr. Frankenstein not been fooled, after all?

But surely, if he knew where we were, Dr. Frankenstein would simply send some guards to collect us. We were in his hands. He had no need for games.

"I really think you should go," Catherine said.

"No doubt you do." Dr. Frankenstein's mellow voice hardened to concrete. "I know who you are. When Angel ripped up the message you had the techie give her, she gave you away. I looked deeper into your background and found out your name was very familiar. You're one of the original birth mothers."

The hairs stood up on the back of my neck.

"Records of surrogate mothers for Project Renaissance were erased. If you recognized my name, it's because you were part of the original project, under the Needham government. You're one of them." Catherine's voice shook with rage. "I was sixteen when you bastards implanted a surgically altered zygote inside me. I couldn't fight you then, but I can now."

"You were paid fifty thousand dollars to bear one of the Renaissance children. Do your underground friends know that?"

"I was sixteen! Too young for the documents I was made to sign to be legal. You made me think I had no choice."

"Your conscience didn't prevent you from taking the money. Or from letting us impregnate you a second time."

Catherine gasped as if in pain. "You'll pay for what you did. My sources say you're going to be fired within the hour."

"Your sources are wrong," Dr. Frankenstein said coolly. "Angel's little demonstration did stir up a bunch of blame-laying higher up. I've been asked to hand in my resignation by nine tomorrow morning or be fired. Which means I have eighteen hours left as project head and I have more than enough power to fire you, effective immediately." A pause. A door opening. "Captain, please escort Ms. Berringer off the premises. And I do mean off the entire Chinchaga site. Her personal belongings will be shipped to her."

Catherine protested loudly and viciously, but

the efficient captain took her away. Dr. Frankenstein left not long afterward.

Mike and I stayed silent for a long fifteen minutes just to be sure. Then Mike put his lips close to my ear. "Wow. You believe them?"

If Dr. Frankenstein knew we were in the next room that scene could have been a hoax staged for our benefit, but I didn't think so. "What would be the point of tricking us?"

"Maybe to get us to track down this supposed underground rescue movement," Mike said.

I nodded to concede the point. "But we have no intention of contacting them, so we might as well proceed as if the escape is real." And I still felt confident that it was real.

Which meant good news: Dr. Frankenstein fired by morning, only eighteen more hours to outfox him.

The hours until we could make our move crept by slowly. Finally, at nine-thirty that evening, when we hadn't heard so much as a footfall for two hours, we decided to go for it.

Avoiding all the cameras would have been impossible, so we slipped out boldly, acting on the assumption that no one would be watching anymore. Or if Dr. Frankenstein was trying to trail us to the underground movement he would have to allow us a fair amount of rope.

We had argued during the wait about where we should go first. Mike favored stocking up on food and then making a run for it. "If we go cross-country we ought to avoid the roadblocks. Unless they've poisoned the water entirely, we should be able to get by for weeks on fish. I have camping gear at home."

Even when I told him about the blackmail Leona had mentioned, he wasn't sure. "We have to search Dr. Frankenstein's office first," I argued. "Just because the good doctor never got around to blackmailing us doesn't mean he didn't have some dirt prepared."

"Secrets, Angel?"

I kissed his palm. "Dr. Frankenstein specializes in disinformation of the incriminating kind. He's already telling the world we're murderers. I don't want any more surprises, do you?"

Finding Dr. Frankenstein's office proved to be the tricky part. The complex had a lot of locked doors and was singularly lacking in directories.

"If you were Dr. Frankenstein, where would you put your office?" I asked Mike in frustration.

"Underground in a crypt?" Mike suggested. "So he can crawl into his coffin every night?"

A smile tugged at my lips. "Near the exercise rooms so he can get up and bike a mile when he has insomnia."

We looked at each other and spoke the same thought: "Near the kitchen."

The rooms adjacent to the kitchen proved to be storage and the furnace, but tucked into a corner of the kitchen itself we found a dumbwaiter, a small service elevator that the cook could place trays of food on and send up to the room above.

I looked at it. "Do you think he's up there?"

Mike's eyebrows quirked. "When there are no cooks in the building? Nah, he's outside coordinating the search."

Our voices sounded loud in the stillness. The building felt deserted, cameras abandoned, but even if someone was radioing frantically for help, it didn't change anything. We still had only a limited window of time. If we were going to search Dr. Frankenstein's office, we had to do it now.

I crawled inside the tiny cage, and Mike sent the dumbwaiter up. If I heard voices we could still retreat and be saved the trouble of getting through the lock on his door.

I heard no voices, and the panel at the top slid open easily. I slithered out headfirst onto the floor, then sent the cage back down for Mike.

The room was dark, with only a tiny bit of illumination coming from under the door. "Lights?" I asked Mike when he joined me.

He shook his head, still wary. We were inside the lion's den. Dr. Frankenstein could have armed his office with motion detectors for all we knew. He was the secretive type.

I followed the edge of the desk in front of me and sat down in the large padded chair. I started opening drawers. Most were locked, but the one directly in front of me slid out at a touch.

It was a computer keyboard. The keys were flat squares instead of raised buttons, and there was a whole set of keys that I didn't know the function of, but it was still very obviously a keyboard.

The question was, where was the screen?

I searched the desktop in case it was recessed into the wood, checked for a TV like the first Texas Instruments computers, hit the return key on the keyboard several times. Nothing happened.

That was all right. What I really wanted was computer disks anyway. I tried more of the drawers but couldn't find the body of the computer or the disk drives, much less any disks, not even the new 3 1/2-inch kind I'd seen in TV commercials.

Frustrated, I leaned back against the chair's headrest, and a visor tipped down over my eyes.

I was so startled I let out a little squeak but quickly calmed down. Through the visor I could see a holographic image of an office as if I were standing inside it. Various items in the office glowed blue: a fishing net hung on the wall, a notepad and pen on the table, a landscape painting, a chest, one door labeled Kitchen and another Living Room, a spinning globe on the desk, and more.

It took me a moment to figure out that this *was* the computer screen. Apple II's familiar] prompt was sadly missing. The image on the screen looked vaguely like some kind of computer game, but there was no joystick, and the arrow keys didn't work.

I brushed my arm against the chair arm, and the image in front of me rotated an alarming 180 degrees. I found myself staring at a wall I hadn't seen before. This door said Library.

I fumbled with the chair arm and discovered a tiny ball bearing that, when I rolled it under my finger, turned the holograph.

That was all. No buttons to push, no way of walking through any of the mysterious doors.

I flipped up the visor, restoring my dim view of Dr. Frankenstein's real office. "This is hopeless. It would take me ten hours to learn how to operate this thing."

Mike wasn't listening; he was poking around Dr. Frankenstein's shelves and opening up his filing cabinet. The cabinet would be the logical place to put files, but the fact that they weren't locked discouraged me.

"This drawer's stuck," Mike said, grunting. "Can you give me a hand?"

It was a large drawer, the height of my knees and fairly wide. Mike had managed to pull it open far enough for us to insert our fingers, but it was definitely stuck.

"On the count of three: one, two, three!"

We heaved together, and the drawer popped open with a loud screech, running over my toes.

I swore, hopped backward, and bruised my hip on the edge of the table. "That *hurts.*"

"What a whiner," Mike said absently. "I want to see what's inside." He stuck his hand in, feeling around for a moment. Then a strange expression came over his face, and he pulled back, staring at his hand. Filaments of something clung to his fingers. "Angel, hit the lights."

"But—"

"Hit them!"

I turned the lights on, blinking in their fluorescent hardness, and looked in the drawer.

I almost threw up. The filaments were strands of brown hair. They were stuck to Mike's hand with blood. He must have touched her face when he reached inside. Leona's face. She hadn't escaped in the missing aircar after all. She was curled up inside the cramped drawer, unnaturally still, head bleeding, arms and legs bound.

CHAPTER

17

"Oh, God." I thought Leona was dead, and I unconsciously started to pray. The drawer was far too small for a human being, obscene in some way, like trying to cram a baby back inside the womb. It was her hipbone that had made the drawer stick. I wanted to throw up again but held back with an effort of will.

"Help me get her out of here." Mike was already reaching inside. The two of us strained to lift her. How had that fiend fit her inside?

I had not the slightest doubt in my mind as to who the fiend was or that he'd put her there deliberately for Mike and me to find.

We laid her out on the floor, and she groaned.

"She's alive!" Mike's voice held the same elation that was pumping through me. "We have to get her some water."

There was no water, but Dr. Frankenstein had equipped his office with a miniature Coke machine—probably another antique—and I quickly popped a can open.

Mike had brushed the hair back out of Leona's face and was pressing a pad of cloth torn from his T-shirt to the cut on her forehead. She looked desperately pale, her eyelids still closed and faintly bruised.

I touched the cold can to her cheek, and she flinched. "Wake up, Leona," I pleaded. "Hurry, he might come back."

Her eyes opened. She looked dazed but alarmed. Mike had pulled the gag from her mouth, and her first word turned a cold dagger in my heart. "Vincent . . ."

Involuntarily, my eyes went to the Coke machine.

Mike sprang up and opened it, but it contained only soda pop. He looked around, then shook his head. There was no space left in the office big enough to conceal a human being.

I held the Coke can to Leona's lips, supporting her head. "Shhh, don't try to talk now. Have something to drink."

She slurped noisily, shuddering at the bite of carbonic acid. Her hands moved to hold the can, but they were still bound. Mike produced a pair of scissors from the desk and started snipping. Dr. Frankenstein had bound her with masking tape. It wasn't as durable as handcuffs, but it was a hell of a lot harder on the circulation. When Leona tried to move, she gasped in pain. "My leg!"

It was lying at an unnatural angle, obviously

broken. Mike gingerly straightened it. Her face paled even more, and she bit her bottom lip.

I mouthed swearwords. "Why did he do this to you?"

The alarm sprang back into her eyes, and she pushed the Coke can away. "There's no time. You have to hurry."

We weren't going to get very far until Leona had recovered enough to walk. Besides, if Dr. Frankenstein had been confident enough to hide Leona here, he must have known where we were. I should have known it was too quiet, too easy.

"Thin people tend to underestimate fat people," he had said. "They associate physical bulk with mental slowness."

He probably had a dozen guards ready to move in the second we opened the door. No, that didn't fit. Even soldiers would protest his treatment of Leona. This was some plan of Dr. Frankenstein's alone.

"Vincent," Leona said again.

"Don't worry, we'll find him," Mike reassured her. The hardness in his face equaled my own. Frankenstein would pay for this.

Leona coughed up a mouthful of pop. "You don't understand. He's holding Vincent prisoner. My brother is the prize in his treasure hunt."

"What?" Mike said sharply.

She coughed again. "This is a treasure hunt. A contest between you and him."

"A treasure hunt?" I didn't get it.

"He hates you. He hates all of us, all the

Renaissance children, but especially you, Angel. He wants revenge for all the years you played dumb and left him looking like a fool in front of his superiors. He blames you for the fact that his career has gone down the tubes."

I remembered "Uncle Albert" becoming so furious he couldn't talk when I beat him in some small skirmish. His eyes had been hot enough to burn coal. I had no trouble believing that he hated me.

"He left you a message on the computer," Leona said.

"How do we operate it?" I asked, seating myself in the chair again.

"It responds to voice commands." Leona closed her eyes. "Say 'Treasure hunt.'"

I flipped the visor down. "Treasure hunt."

A small chest in one corner of the blue virtual office expanded, and Dr. Frankenstein's recorded voice began to play.

"Project Renaissance is over, its funding cut, all the employees laid off. I've sent the military away on a fruitless search. We're all alone. It's just you and me now, and I want a rematch." He sounded smug.

"I have daVincible Vincent"—Leona began to cry—"and Leonardo has been incapacitated. That still leaves it two against one. You have all the advantages. So let's have it out once and for all. Michelangelo against Frankenstein, *renascentia* versus *sapiens*, in a battle to the death— your death, of course. I've set you a little treasure hunt. You have two hours to complete it or I'll slit Vincent's throat. If you find me in less than two hours I'll let you go free. If you run overtime I kill you all. The clock started running at ten o'clock. If it took you a little longer to find my office, too bad."

The recording ended.

I looked at my watch. It was 10:31 already.

"Please." Leona grabbed my wrists. "You have to help Vincent. I know you don't like me, but you have to help us."

I patted her hand. "Of course we will. Quick, what's the first clue?"

"No," Mike interrupted suddenly. "Angel and I don't have to do anything. How do we know Vincent's really in danger? You've been on Dr. Frankenstein's side all along. This is just another setup like the badminton tournament."

Leona's face spasmed.

Mike was right, I was chagrined to realize. She wasn't telling us the truth—or at least not all of it.

Leona removed the pad from her forehead. "This is real blood," she said. "And my leg is really broken. Dr. Frankenstein made me stand while he broke it with some kind of gadget. He said if I flinched he might accidentally sever my artery and wouldn't that be too bad? He made Vincent stuff me into the drawer, when every jostle hurt so much I had to fight to stop myself from screaming—and Vincent knew it. He made my brother cry. Do you think we would willingly have let that happen if we'd had a choice? Vincent is in real danger. Dr. Frankenstein will kill him if you don't solve the treasure hunt."

"But you do know more than you're telling us," Mike said softly.

Leona looked ready to scream. "There isn't time—"

Mike sat down on Dr. Frankenstein's desk, arms folded. "Make time. Angel and I aren't going anywhere until you tell us everything."

I resisted the urge to look at my watch. I believed Leona when she said Dr. Frankenstein would kill Vincent, but I had to back up Mike.

"All right," Leona said swiftly, "the badminton tournament was a setup. Vincent and I knew that, but we didn't know there would be bullets flying. Dr. Frankenstein didn't tell us that part or we wouldn't have been there. He used Erin Reinders's baby to blackmail us into helping him at the tournament. Just like later he blackmailed us into—" She clamped her mouth shut.

"Into what?" I asked.

Mike held up his watch, a silent warning that time was running out. My nails dug into my palms, waiting for Leona to crack.

"You fool," Leona said. "He's listening to us right now. If I tell you, I don't know what he'll do to Vincent, don't you understand?"

"I understand that Dr. Frankenstein has a powerful desire to see us running around like chickens with their heads cut off solving some treasure hunt. I don't want to do what he wants. You have to convince me." Mike's expression remained hard.

"He blackmailed Vincent into going with one of his customers."

"Customers?" A prickle went up my spine.

"The purpose of the original top-secret Needham government project was to create perfect weapons. Superspies. Agents to use in Limited Wars. Assassins. Elite soldiers. Us." Leona spoke so fast she stumbled over the words. "When the Needham government fell, Dr. Frankenstein decided it would be more profitable to sell us to the highest bidder.

"Not all of us died in the Orphanage fire or escaped. Some of us were only made to look as though we'd escaped. Some of us were illegally sold to powers that have very advanced brainwashing techniques and no scruples.

"He's rented Vincent out once already to some terrorist faction. Vincent won't talk about what they made him do, but I know it was bad. Dr. Frankenstein kept me behind as insurance, but he intends to sell us in pairs. Breeding pairs, he calls them." Leona laughed, an ugly sound. "He says Vincent isn't really my twin or even my brother. Maybe he's telling the truth and maybe he isn't. It doesn't matter. Vincent is my twin because we say he is." Fierce determination shone briefly through her pain and fear.

"What about Mike and me?" I asked. The word "rented" struck a chill in my heart. "Has he sold us, too?"

"Not yet. His customers are quite canny. Dr. Frankenstein didn't get the proof that you were what he said you were until you tackled Dave Belcourt. Since then he's been negotiating with two groups, iBankCon and a tobacco company, driving the price up and up."

"If the Renaissance children are so valuable, why would he kill Vincent?" Mike asked.

"Because of the riot Angel staged. He was quite pleased with it at first. He saw it as more proof of your abilities. But it backfired on him: he's been fired. His customers are refusing to pay, saying he can no longer promise delivery. They think they'll be able to pick us up more cheaply when we're free of him." Leona looked so pale I was afraid she would pass out again. "Dr. Frankenstein has lost everything, and he blames us. You have to save Vincent. You damn well have to."

Mike and I exchanged glances. I believed Leona. "All right, we'll do it. But you have to take care of our other problem." I spoke in code for the benefit of any hidden listeners and held Leona's gaze, willing her to understand.

She held her hands in front of her face as if holding a camera and depressed an invisible shutter. "Gotcha."

Message received. On to the next order of business. "What's the first clue?"

She looked blank.

"Treasure hunts always have clues," I said. My mother had made up hunts for my birthday. Things like, Go seven paces north, then twice that number west, and look under the white rock. Somehow I doubted that Dr. Frankenstein's clues would be so easy to follow. "Didn't he say anything else?"

Leona shook her head. "No."

I glanced at my watch: 10:43. "Are you sure he didn't say anything else, Leona? Anything at all?"

She shook her head in despair.

"Did he do anything?"

"No, he—" She paused, frowning. "He stuck something to the door."

Mike was at the door in an instant, using the same lightning reflexes he'd used on the badminton court. I could feel my own adrenaline pumping. He peeled something off the door. "It's a yellow sticky note."

"What does it say?" I crowded closer and looked for myself. The sticky note didn't say anything; it had a pattern of arrows drawn on it pointing diagonally up. "Put it back on the door exactly where it was."

He did so, and I traced the path of the arrow up to the ceiling and discovered another arrow-covered sticky note. This one pointed to the right.

Mike and I followed the arrows quickly as they zigzagged around the room and then out the door and into the hallway. The next one led to the elevator and pointed at the level three button. I was afraid the elevator would be rigged or wouldn't work, but it delivered us to the correct floor without demanding a security key.

The trail finally came to a halt in a bathroom, stuck to a toilet seat. The last sticky note didn't have an arrow. It said: "You've just wasted four minutes following a red herringbone."

I took a closer look at the stickies and felt sick to my stomach. The pattern *was* herringbone, not arrows. "That cheater. That sniveling—"

"We don't have time for that," Mike snapped, his anger directed at Dr. Frankenstein, not me. "Of course, he set traps. He doesn't want us to win. Think. If the clue isn't the arrows, it must be the medium, the yellow sticky note itself. Where do you find yellow stickies?"

"In a drugstore." I was determined not to rush ahead of myself this time. "Or anyone's desk."

"A drugstore," Mike said. "He'll want to spread the hunt all over town to cost us traveling time."

We sprinted down the hallway, back to the waiting elevator. Mike hit L for Lobby. We had a smooth ride up, and we raced for the front doors. They stood open and unlocked— unguarded. The hairs prickled on the back of my neck, but no one stopped us, and we pushed through the glass double doors into the night.

It was cold out; a breeze frisked and nipped around us. Today was the first of November; we were lucky there wasn't any snow. All the streetlights were on, but most of the houses were dark. Even the ones with lit windows were silent. No TVs playing, no shadows behind the drawn curtains, no laughter, no traffic.

A ghost town.

We were in Chinchaga. My guess had been correct. Mike and I swung right, following the riverbank. The park where Mike and I had first met was only a block away.

We ran hard, speaking in compressed sentences.

"Look out for a car."

"He'll cheat."

But we found no car innocently abandoned on the street with keys dangling from the ignition, and knowing Dr. Frankenstein would cheat was no help. He still had Vincent. We still had to go after him and hope that we were smarter in the end than he was.

I didn't feel smart. The drugstore was just one guess out of possible dozens. A yellow sticky note might mean gold glue, for all I knew. The office desk theory could be right, but there were a lot of offices.

We ran, turning onto Main Street, the highway through town. Most of the businesses were on First Avenue, but the drugstore squatted halfway down Main Street, between the town hall and a flower shop.

Most of the hunt would probably take place here. There were too many strangers' houses to search. If Dr. Frankenstein was being even slightly fair—and I thought his pride would demand it— he had limited himself to three dozen businesses around the core and a few other public places like the hospital or the school.

Mike jerked at the drugstore door. It was locked. He kicked at the glass, meaning to break it.

I thought of Mike punching through the window, cutting an artery and bleeding to death on the pavement. Leona's leg was broken. No one would come.

Mike put his shoulder to the door, crashing against it. Without looking at my watch, I knew it was about five minutes to eleven. One hour left and God knows how many clues to come.

"Wait!" There was one car on the street, a black Chevrolet. I tried all the doors. The third one opened. I swarmed through into the driver's seat. The keys were in the ignition. God bless model towns with no crime.

The engine turned over, and I backed up illegally. Mike leaped out of the way, and I aimed the black hood at the drugstore doors, smashing them open.

I succeeded better than I had intended, and for a second I thought the whole building would come down around me in a torrent of bricks. Without waiting to see if it would or not, I backed up again, put the car in Park, and jumped out.

Mike was already running through the twisted doorframe. He flicked on the lights, and we headed for the aisle with paper and pens and other office supplies.

I found the Post-it notes in the center of the aisle, next to boxes of size 10 business envelopes. We tore through the sticky notes frantically, but they were all still wrapped in plastic, crinkly and undisturbed.

Dead end. Dr. Frankenstein would be grinning. Laughing. He had a sick sense of humor.

"Post-it notes," I said. "Post-it, not yellow stickies."

Mike understood at once. We didn't even speak as we ran out of the drugstore, knocking down magazine stands and not pausing. We jumped into the car, Mike driving this time, and whipped over half a block to the post office.

The post office doors could be accessed only by steps; it was impossible to drive a car up them. "Don't be locked, don't be locked," I chanted.

The doors were open. I pushed through, into a room with rows of locked silver boxes. No white note, no yellow stickies, only another set of doors. Locked this time. You could pick up your mail anytime at night, but the rest of the building was shut tighter than a drum.

Mike smacked his hand against the thick glass in frustration. "We need another battering ram."

"Maybe there's a back door," I said, already pushing back outside.

Mike caught me on the steps. In the yellow sodium light his grin was manic and reckless. "How about the parcel drop?"

It was a steel drawer, not a slot, designed to accommodate bulky parcels, but it was too small for a human being. A thirteen-year-old gymnast might have fit through it but not me. "Impossible."

Mike put his foot in the drawer and stood on it, steadying himself against the ceiling. *Screeeeech!* His weight bent the metal down out of the way.

I didn't give myself time to think about it, just stuck my head inside and started squirming through, collecting bruises like stamps.

Mike boosted me, and I accidentally kicked him in the chest before falling inside. I tucked into a somersault to protect my head, but the room wasn't very big, and my legs crunched against a wall.

It was very dark, and it took me another minute to fight my way out of the back room, past the front counter to the doors. Fumbling along the wall brought illumination. I unlocked the dead bolt and let Mike in.

"You take the back, I'll take the front," Mike said, already ducking under the counter, moving toward the cash register and the parcel scale. "Look for a weapon while you're at it."

I went past him, into the back, where the open postal boxes gaped. Stacks of mail were piled along the counter, ready for sorting.

Should we search the bag? No, that would take ages.

Or should we search the boxes? Most of them contained mail.

My gaze sharpened. Written on tape over each slot was a name and number. Dr. Frankenstein would think it humorous to address the note to us.

Three rows down and two columns over from the right I found it: box 601, Michelangelo. It contained three flyers, two large envelopes, and a letter from M. Shelley.

Mary Shelley, author of *Frankenstein*. I ripped it open. "Mike, come here."

He read the letter over my shoulder. It was a poem. Of sorts.

'Twas nighttime and the rotten kids
Did sweat and tremble in the draft.
All loosened were their bowels,
And the clever genius laughed.

Beware the ticking clock, my foe,
The hands that glide, the arms that sweep.
Beware the seventh sin and tend
The crafty fat old creep.

As before, the words were just insults, window dressing. The form was the clue.

"It reminds me of something," I said. "Some other poem I've read. In English class, maybe. Especially that one line, 'Beware the ticking clock, my foe.'"

"'The jaws that bite, the claws that catch,'" Mike said abruptly.

I looked at him in surprise as he pulled me out of the room. "''Twas brillig, and the slithy toves Did gyre and gimble in the wabe,'" he quoted. "Lewis Carroll. 'Beware the Jabberwock, my son.' The next clue has to be in the library somewhere."

My watch said 11:20. No time to stop and argue other theories about toilets (bowels) and clocks. We could only gamble, grinding away from the curb in the still-running Chevy, doing an evil two-point turn in the middle of the road. Race to the library.

"Which one? School or public?" I yelled, screeching to a stop at the junction with Main Street. Left or right?

"Wait a second," Mike said. "This is wrong. The treasure hunt is another test, just like the others. It's a demonstration for Dr. Frankenstein's customers, a sales pitch. They'll be ready to take delivery as soon as we prove ourselves."

"I know," I said. I'd known as soon as Leona mentioned companies and foreign powers bidding on Renaissance children. "So which way, school or public?"

"You knew?" Mike echoed. "If you knew, what are we doing here?"

"Public library," I decided, turning right. "He'd use a different clue for the school." I floored the accelerator, driving up the street. "It doesn't matter," I told Mike. "Leona's working on the customers—we can deal with them later. It's Dr. Frankenstein we have to beat now. Do you want him to win?"

"No. But—"

We reached the library. I didn't bother to get out and check the library doors—the good doctor would have made sure they were locked—I drove straight through, bumping to a halt against some interior steps.

I threw open my door and got out of the car. Mike swore but followed me. He said no more about the customers—he knew as well as I that they were likely watching us right now via satellite, that all the clue spots would be bugged.

Mike headed for the children's section and the *C*'s while I tried the card catalog. It would be just like Dr. Frankenstein to hide the clue there instead of in the pages of the book.

"Carroll, Lewis. Use for Dodgson, Charles Lutwidge." I flipped through the cards: *Alice's Adventures in Wonderland, The Hunting of the Snark, Through the Looking-Glass*. No "Jabberwocky."

Ten feet away from me Mike was tossing children's books on the floor, the same titles I'd named. He shook his head; he hadn't found anything either.

" 'Jabberwocky' " was a poem. Maybe it was in a collection of poems. I sprinted over to the index tables and the poetry index, looked it up with shaking fingers. "Beware the ticking clock, my foe." Dead ends, dead ends, dead ends.

" 'Jabberwocky,' " the entry read. "Poem by Lewis Carroll in Chapter One of *Through the Looking-Glass and What Alice Found There*."

" 'Jabberwocky' is in one of the books." I shouted the title to Mike.

He snatched the book up off the floor and began pawing frantically through the illustrations. "The poem's in mirror writing."

I was on my feet. "The bathroom." The only mirror in a library.

Mike started to follow, but I stopped him. "No. Keep reading in case this is a dead end. Have you checked the inside pocket?"

I hadn't been in the library often enough to know where the bathrooms were. It took me another sixty seconds—"the hands that glide"—before I found them in the basement. Ladies and Gentlemen.

Nothing behind either mirror. Nothing

scratched on the surface. Nothing in the toilet bowls.

"The arms that sweep."

Back upstairs, I shook my head at Mike's expression. "Find anything? What does the poem mean?"

"I don't know. Humpty Dumpty's explaining it to Alice, but it doesn't make any sense to me. It's a nonsense poem. Carroll made up words by packing two words into one. 'Slithy' means 'lithe' and 'slimy.'" He turned several pages, skimming. "No good. She talks to the White King next."

"Humpty Dumpty knows, but we don't. 'Humpty Dumpty sat on a wall, Humpty Dumpty had a great fall. All the king's horses and all the king's men couldn't put Humpty Dumpty together again.' That's a big help."

"Mother Goose?" Mike suggested, just as I said, "Eggs. The grocery store."

Two possible solutions again, and maybe both were wrong. "Grab the books," I said. "You can read them in the car."

The grocery store sounded right to me. Dr. Frankenstein's level of humor.

"'Simple Simon,' 'Four and Twenty Blackbirds,' 'Jack and Jill,'" Mike muttered as I screeched around the corner. "This is stupid," he complained, slamming the book shut. "I don't understand why we're doing this. If it's a demonstration, Dr. Frankenstein won't kill Vincent."

"Oh, yes, he will." The car bumped over a

curb. "Remember the missing aircar? Dr. Frankenstein killed an innocent guard just to draw off the military. If we lose the treasure hunt in front of his customers, we have no value and Dr. Frankenstein will kill Vincent." In the I.G.A. parking lot I banged into an abandoned shopping cart. It got hooked on the fender and dragged along after us, squealing.

"And if we win?" Mike asked, bracing himself against the dashboard.

"Dr. Frankenstein will kill us anyhow to prove that he can." I rammed through the double doors of the supermarket, finally dislodging the cart from the car bumper.

The hood of the car crumpled, and Mike and I were thrown forward against our seat belts. I had a bad feeling about the noise the engine was making, but there was no time to look at it.

Without pause, we got out of the car and went inside. Some dim lights were on at the back of the store, so we didn't bother searching for switches. We just ran hell-bent past the produce section, past the cracker and cereal aisle toward the milk and eggs.

I knew the layout from shopping trips for my mother and turned without looking into aisle 7.

My right foot slipped, and I went down in a greasy skid on my hands and knees. Wet goo coated my hands; I tried to push myself up and slipped back down, skinning my elbow. Something crackled underneath my knee.

Mike had managed to keep from stepping in the goo, warned by my fall. Disgust bunched up his face. "It's egg yolk. Raw eggs." He gave me a hand up: without it I would have fallen again.

The entire aisle was a runny mess of slimy eggs from end to end, sprinkled here and there with broken eggshells.

The goo started to dry and harden on my jeans; I could feel egg white in my hair, on my arms up to the elbow. I was furious with myself for not having been more cautious.

One side of the aisle held freezers full of waffles and pastry; on the other side were the eggs, cheese, and milk. I put one foot into the low cheese bin that ran the length of the aisle, intending to avoid the egg-slick floor.

"Wait!" Mike pointed, and I saw that Dr. Frankenstein had been very clever indeed.

Sitting on the very top shelf halfway down the aisle was a single egg. A face and a suit had been drawn on it with a black marker. Humpty Dumpty—balanced on the very edge of the top shelf.

The threat was obvious. If we jostled the shelves and the egg fell, we might lose the clue. "All the king's horses and all the king's men couldn't put Humpty together again."

We would have to do this the hard way.

We waded out into the broken eggs.

Even watching where I placed my feet, I fell once more and got pulled down another time trying to hold Mike up, sliding and squishing, like comic movie villains foiled by a kid and a bag of marbles. But it wasn't funny, and we weren't the villains.

The soles of my shoes were so coated with egg that it became easier to skate than walk. We made it safely to the center of the aisle and Humpty.

Mike jumped up and plucked the egg from its perch as if blocking a basketball shot. He lost his balance on the landing, quickly tossing the egg to me before he crashed.

I caught it, didn't crush it, studied it carefully.

"Well?" Mike hauled himself up again.

"There's something written on it." I turned the egg toward the paltry light source and saw letters running along Humpty's belt. We would never have been able to reconstruct the shell if Humpty had fallen. The clue read, "leap off the cliff leap off the cliff"

CHAPTER

18

"Let me see."

I gave the egg to Mike for him to pore over. The words circled in my head just as they circled Humpty Dumpty's body.

"leap off the cliff leap off the cliff"

The message contained no capital letters and no periods. Had Dr. Frankenstein done that on purpose? What was the true clue—the cliff leap off? off the cliff leap? cliff leap off the? Nothing seemed to change the meaning; it still seemed to refer to Humpty taking a high dive.

The shelf wasn't exactly a cliff, though. I ran through some synonyms: "cliff," "precipice," "bluff."

" 'Escarpment,' " Mike said. " 'Palisade.' "

" 'Riverbank. Bank.' " A bank was also a building. "Bank leap. Bank vault.' "

A spark leaped between Mike's eyes and mine. "Bank vault! That's it. Good going, that's our fastest solve time yet." He didn't add that we needed it. The clock stood at 11:35. We had twenty-five minutes left, and we'd solved only three clues. I didn't know how many clues were left, but I was sure Dr. Frankenstein would have made more than three.

To avoid the slippery floor Mike climbed into the bin with the cheeses and scrambled through them back to the front of the store. I followed, scraped at my dripping shoes, then hopped back to the ground. Solid, dry floor, bless it.

We took off as if from a gun.

Halfway through the store Mike veered down the housewares aisle. He caught up with me outside. "Steak knives," he said, tossing a package to me. "I still say Frankenstein won't kill us in front of witnesses, but—"

"They're not witnesses," I gasped. "They're his audience." Dr. Frankenstein needed to prove his superiority to somebody.

I paused a microsecond before getting into the car. "Which bank?" Chinchaga boasted three. CIBC was the closest, so we could count it out—unless Dr. Frankenstein was playing reverse psychology.

Mike didn't stop, mentally ahead of me. "Alberta Treasury Branch." He revved the engine.

Treasure hunt, treasury branch. Very cute. I tore at the steak knives' plastic wrapping with my teeth.

Mike backed up, and something squealed under the crunched-up hood. No matter. We were still mobile. Mike bumped across a rut-ridden alley and gunned for the Alberta Treasury Branch.

It took me a few seconds to realize he was aiming at the building on the left. I yanked on the wheel. "That's the liquor store!"

We careened the other way but hit our target. The alarms went off as we crashed through the doors of the Treasury Branch, jangling my nerves so that I was already out of the car before I realized the Chevy's engine had died. The hood was crumpled worse than any demolition-derby car I'd seen.

Not a good sign.

Inside the bank, I jumped the long curved counter and headed for the vault in the corner.

It was locked, of course, the thick steel door shut, the heavy bolts in place. "Look for the combination," Mike said. There were two com-bination locks numbered from 0 to 99, a secu-rity feature, I presumed, requiring two people to open the vault. Mike bent over the one on the left. "Maybe the actor playing the manager wrote it down in a drawer inside their desk or something. What's your birth date?"

"December 7, 1970. Or 2081, depending." Between terminals on the teller counter were rows of drawers. I yanked open the nearest one. Deposit slips, forms, pencils, pens, gold name tags. I lifted the pencil tray but didn't find even the faintest of pencil markings. The next three columns of drawers were virtually identical, not even yielding a button to shut off the alarm.

I wondered why they had bothered to install a security system when there was no real money in the bank and no police to storm to the rescue when the alarm went off. Historical accuracy, I supposed.

"What's Michelangelo's birthday?"

"How should I know? Try the other two words in the clue—'off the.'" I abandoned the tellers' counter and ducked into the Plexiglas cage in the center of the room. I found cash there—this was where the tellers got it from during the day, not the vault—but no combination. I almost ripped a cupboard door off the shelf, then scanned its contents rapidly. Weren't there any lazybones in this bank?

Next drawer.

On the countertop were three pens; two pencils and six erasers had been arranged to spell $A = 24$. Relief shuddered through me; I had to clutch the counter while I called to Mike. "Vincent left us a clue. $A = 24$."

If you numbered the letters of the alphabet, then shifted those numbers to the right until A was the twenty-fourth letter, O-F-F-T-H-E became—

"12, 3, 3, 17, 5, 2," Mike said. "I used to do codes as a kid. But I can't dial two threes in a row."

I moved up beside him. "Try 12, 33, 17, 52."

Left, right, left, right. Turn to 0.

The tumbler clicked, and I started trying combinations on the second lock. But 12, 33, 17, 52 didn't work—that would have been too easy.

Neither did 52, 17, 33, 12. My fingers began to
sweat, slipping on the dial, and I was about to
yell at Mike to stop crowding me when my third
try—13, 23, 15, 72, using every second digit—
did the trick.

Click.

Mike turned the wheel on the door, and the
bolts slid back into the door. He shoved the
vault open and stepped into the long narrow
room.

I started to follow but saw the vault door start
to swing shut and barely caught it in time. The
door was hollow but heavy, eight inches thick,
with bolts as thick as my wrist.

The alarm screamed inside my brain. "Beware
the seventh sin and tend . . ." The seventh deadly
sin was sloth. Had we saved enough time? It was
11:48 now.

I was afraid Dr. Frankenstein might have hidden the next clue in one of the safe-deposit
boxes, but apparently he hadn't bothered, confident that the combination would take us
hours—and without Vincent's clue it would
have.

Mike came out carrying a piece of white
paper, and we scrammed out of the building. We
jumped into the car and read the clue by street-
light, to the tune of the strident alarm.

"You haven't got a chance."

More negative psychology. I looked at the
form of the message again, but it was just plain
white paper, nothing special, no creases on it,
no words whited out, no watermark.

Mike shifted into Park and tried to start the engine. It whined horribly but refused to turn over. "Ten minutes. He's right; we don't have a prayer." The bank vault clue had taken us thirteen minutes, the Humpty clue twenty-two minutes.

"Think," I insisted. *Whine, whine, screech.* " 'You haven't got a chance.' " I brainstormed out loud. "Chance, luck, gambling." But there were no casinos in Chinchaga. I couldn't even think of a bingo hall. "Lottery tickets?"

"Maybe." Mike grabbed my arm before I could jump out of the car wreck. "Wait. We have to think. If this is the last clue we can't run into it blindly. He'll have set a trap; he'll cheat. This is to the death."

"Vincent—"

"Getting ourselves killed won't help Vincent," Mike said brutally. "That's presuming Dr. Frankenstein hasn't killed him already."

"No. He won't do that." I shook my head, positive on that point. "Not before midnight. His pride won't let him." Pride was the whole reason for this contest. Dr. Frankenstein had grown up fat and repulsive; he'd tried to make a virtue out of a fault, telling himself his weight didn't matter because he was intelligent—very intelligent, a genius. In his whole life he'd never met anyone smarter than he was; being outwitted by a couple of sarcastic teenagers threatened his worldview.

"Are you so sure your own pride isn't involved?" Mike asked. "He has a gun, and we have steak knives. Logic says we lose."

"What are you saying? That we should abandon Vincent?"

Mike was silent for a second, trying the engine again with no luck. "You think he'd ride to our rescue?"

I didn't, but I didn't think Vincent would believe we'd come after him, either. "Dr. Frankenstein locked Leona up in a drawer." The words were pulled out of my tight throat. "As if she was a thing, not a human being. Dave didn't think we were human either. Like Mr. Lindstrom calling Carl a robot. I am a human being, and I will not let another human being die if I can possibly help it."

Mike gave a curt nod. Subject closed. "All right, we'll try, but I still think we're dead in the water. Even if we beat Dr. Frankenstein, his clients will be waiting in the wings." A sudden arrested expression came over his face. "Dead in the water. 'You haven't got a chance.' That's what the clue means. He's at the pool."

"Or 'You haven't got a prayer.' Could be a church," I said.

We looked at each other. "Pool," we said together, scrambling out of the car. I was beginning to get a feel for how Dr. Frankenstein's mind worked, and the gruesome image evoked in "Dead in the water" struck a chord. Mike and I set off at a dead run.

My mind worked ferociously, fueled by every pounding stride, and by the time we neared the pool—at 11:54—I had a plan. Of sorts.

"We'll stage a two-pronged attack. I go in and

talk; you kill the lights at midnight on the dot, so the customers are in the dark about who's winning. Then you come in fast and silent."

Mike understood instantly, just as Leona had. "You play dead for the cameras. But why you and not me?" A little machismo had rubbed off on him, after all.

"Can you run faster than I can?" I demanded in a whisper, kicking off my shoes.

Mike followed suit. "No, but—"

"Are you stronger than I am on the badminton court? Do I tire faster than you or return shots more weakly?" I balanced on one foot, then the other, peeling off my socks.

"No."

"But every other girl you've ever met does, right?" I stood there in my bare feet, not even noticing the rough pavement. "It's a fact of life; you can see it in the Olympics. Women compete only with one another because on average men are stronger. *Sapiens* men are stronger than *sapiens* women are. But Renaissance men and women are equal. If I go in there, Dr. Frankenstein can't help but underestimate me."

Dr. Frankenstein hated me more than he hated Mike because, more than anything, he resented being beaten by a girl.

"Maybe," Mike said.

I brought out the big guns. "This afternoon you said you trusted me. Have you lost faith in me already?"

Silence.

"I'm putting my life in your hands, Mike,

trusting you to hit the lights at exactly the right time. Please trust me to distract Dr. Frankenstein."

Mike swore, caught. He kissed me hard and pushed me toward the door. "I'll do the lights. Go."

I held the steak knife against my leg and crept into the darkened building, following the smell of chlorine. As always, the tiles underfoot were wet, chill. I stripped off my egg-stiff jeans. Best not to be hampered by them if there was any possibility of going in the water.

Dead in the water.

Dr. Frankenstein intended to leave our bodies floating in the pool.

Past the change stalls, ghosting through the showers, out to the pool.

The underwater lights glowed, showing the lane lines and a black shape under the diving board, ten meters down, unmoving. Vincent.

Dr. Frankenstein had cheated, after all.

I'm sorry, Leona.

"It's 11:57," Dr. Frankenstein said, stepping out of the shadows by the bleachers. "Not quite midnight. Better hurry, though, your friend is getting low on oxygen."

The shapes beside Vincent resolved into a large black weight and an oxygen tank.

"I told him there was enough oxygen to last until midnight, but I knew he would breathe shallowly so I put in less. I'm amazed he's lasted this long."

I could see the gun in Dr. Frankenstein's pudgy hands.

"Drop your weapon," Dr. Frankenstein said. "I'm sure you have one by now."

I let the steak knife fall and clatter.

"Very good. Now step away from it." I obeyed. "And where's your other little friend, Angel? Tell Mike to go ahead and step out. You still have three minutes left, but it'll take both of you to lift the weight. Come on in, Mike. Don't be shy."

"He's at the church," I lied. "We couldn't decide what the clue meant. We split up."

"You're lying, but that's okay. You two go ahead and try whatever you're planning. I'm ready." His watch beeped. "Now it's 11:58. Go for a dip, Angel. I'll watch."

The moment I dived into the pool I would be signing my own death warrant. No matter how excellent the swimmer, a person on land could walk faster, could move quickly, while the swimmer had to push through liquid. Being in the water would be like being trapped in taffy. I would be helpless.

"No." I took a step back. "I can't swim."

"What a little liar you are. I almost believe you could become an actress. But you're testing your talents on the wrong man. I know your record, remember? You got your Bronze Cross this summer. You swim like a fish."

Everything fell into place as if predestined to be there.

"If you've seen my records, then you'll know I almost drowned this summer," I lashed out. "Mike pulled me out of the pool unconscious. I haven't been back in the water since. I can't bear to wade in water over my ankles." I hugged myself. It was cold in the building, despite the heat I could see rising off the pool.

The tiniest flicker of a doubt crossed his face.

"An interesting story," Dr. Frankenstein said. "It would be amusing, if it were true. But it's not. Jump in the pool, Angel." He stepped closer with the gun.

"I'll drown." I moved sideways, away from the door. I wanted Dr. Frankenstein's back to be to it for Mike's entrance. Did Mike's watch have the same time as Dr. Frankenstein's?

I kept backing up.

He followed me, his arms out in front of him like a professional marksman, keeping both entrances and me in his line of sight. "If you don't jump in, you forfeit, and I'll shoot you now."

I broke out in a fresh sweat, shook my head.

Another step.

Another.

I bumped into the diving tower.

In the second that I was distracted, he took a quick step forward and pressed the gun up under my chin. It was a revolver, and it felt huge. I closed my eyes, not having to fake the waves of sickness and fear coming off me. He was close enough for me to strike him or knee him in the crotch, but his finger was curled tight around the trigger. I would be dead before I moved, my throat blown out.

Dr. Frankenstein smiled, eyes empty. He

knew he had me. "Jump in the pool. You still have a minute."

I went up a step.

The gun stayed under my chin, jammed against my throat, making it hard to breathe, and my heart was pumping so fast I needed all the oxygen I could get.

It would be the same for Vincent under all that water, with pounds of pressure on his body. And how long ago had Dr. Frankenstein weighted him down and dropped him over the edge? Half an hour ago, an hour? It would get harder and harder to keep his breathing shallow as the gauge showed less and less oxygen, and he began to panic.

I kept going up. Dr. Frankenstein stayed with me, using one hand to hold on to the ladder and the other to jab the muzzle of the gun into me, not allowing me even the fantasy of falling on him and knocking him off the diving tower.

His watch beeped on the seventh rung up: 11:59.

I began to pray that Mike's watch was close to Dr. Frankenstein's. If the lights went out now, it would be good-bye, Angel.

I was at the top of the steps now. Had I climbed too quickly? Slowly, gingerly, I took one step backward onto the narrow three-meter springboard.

Dr. Frankenstein joined me at the top, breathing a little heavily but with the gun now pointing at my chest. "So which will it be? The pool or a bullet? You can't retreat much farther."

I took another step back.

He followed. "Do you think I'm afraid to come after you? I'm not. I have excellent balance. Will it be the devil or the deep blue sea, Angel?"

"Please." My voice was hoarse. "I can't. The water—I'll drown."

"Oh, you are a fine actress. My mother would have loved you. She was a talent scout for the movies. She lived and breathed cheekbones and stage presence."

He had the gun pressed against my breast-bone now, too close to risk jumping. I glided backward another step. "What kind of movies did your mother make?"

"You're not listening. She didn't make movies; she was a talent scout, not a director." He scowled, and my heart jumped. Reading his mood fluctuations was akin to maintaining a weather watch in tornado season.

"What actors did she scout?" I asked quickly.

"No one that you've heard of." He laughed at his little joke. "She specialized in child actors."

Another careful step backward, feeling with my feet so I didn't step off the end or the sides.

He followed me without thinking, and the board bowed under our combined weight. Would it snap if we went farther?

Any time now, Mike. The gun's muzzle no longer touched me, and I was close enough to the end of the board to dive off. The recoil would probably tip Dr. Frankenstein in, and the gun would get wet and not fire. Unless he had some kind of futuristic laser gun . . .

My mind bounced around like a pinball, divided between strategy and listening closely to what Dr. Frankenstein was saying about his mother.

"I was too fat to be an actor, of course, so she dedicated herself to getting my younger brother on the big screen. Robin was just like you."

I heard the hatred in his voice and shivered. I had an instant picture in my mind of a fat, miserable little boy outshone by his brother, always being nagged by his mother to eat less but eating *more* out of frustration, priding himself on his one talent, his intellect, scorning others for their slower minds just as they scorned him for his obesity. I stepped back—

And there was no place to put my foot. I was at the end. The board wobbled. It was definitely curved down now, straining under its burden, making it harder for me to keep my balance.

Dr. Frankenstein, deep in thoughts of his past, didn't seem to notice my predicament. "Robin was good-looking and graceful but very melodramatic. Always had to be the center of attention." He smiled as if at a pleasant memory. "I remember the day I came home and found him bleeding in the bathtub. He'd slit his wrists. It was so funny. He kept begging me to call an ambulance. 'If you didn't want to die, you shouldn't have cut your wrists,' I told him."

Beep, beep.

Midnight.

Even before the second beep I was bending my knees, starting to spring up for a simple backward swan dive, the kind that looked so graceful on TV—and a bullet plowed through my shoulder, like a hammer swung against flesh, and I fell instead of diving, my form all gone to hell, zero scores for sure; pain wrapped itself around me. As the water rushed up, everything was black—*I'm going to die*—

Impact.

I was still fairly vertical and went deep, the water black, so black, not a speck of light anywhere, chlorine stinging my eyes and my shoulder, scouring the wound. Why did it hurt so much if I was dead? And then I realized that everything was black because Mike had killed the lights.

I had taken a big breath, but I'd lost part of it on impact. I fought the urge to kick my way back up to the surface. There had been no cannonball splash; Dr. Frankenstein had not followed me down. He was still up there, with a gun. I had to convince him he'd killed me, and that meant no splashing or breathing too loud when I resurfaced.

My foot touched bottom, and my downward momentum stopped.

I tried to untense my body, to ignore the pain and drift ever so slowly up to the surface. . . .

My toe dragged across something.

It caught for only a second, but it was enough to remind me: Vincent.

I swam back down, feeling his body frantically with one hand. There. Was his chest rising and falling? I couldn't feel any movement. I moved my hand up to his shoulder and arms. His hands were tied behind his back. They didn't twitch under mine.

Was he dead? He couldn't be. I felt his chest again, while my lungs clawed for air.

Still no movement, damn it. I should have jumped in right away. My position probably wouldn't be any worse than it was now, wounded and in the dark, and Vincent would be alive.

You can't know that. Dr. Frankenstein had reduced Vincent's air supply. It could have run out ten minutes ago while we were at the bank or slipping in egg yolk.

But I still felt guilty for not thinking faster, being smarter. *Sorry, Leona.* Her image flashed into my mind, face pale, stuffed into a drawer—

No. I didn't have time for this. Dr. Frankenstein was coming, looking for me in the dark. He would find me easily by the splash I made coming up for air.

A terrible thought occurred to me: Vincent was dead; if I loosed the weight from around his ankles he would float up and I could use him as a decoy.

Bile threatened, but need overruled. With my fingers I found the rope tied to his feet and fumbled with the knot, eyes burning, lungs heaving for nonexistent air. My fingers were clumsy, my right arm numb and useless.

Air.

I gave up, started to kick off, then felt the rope slip through my fingers. The weight came free, but Vincent didn't float; the air tank must have been too heavy. Blind and close to blacking out, I grabbed at the oxygen tank.

Vincent grabbed back, coming to life underneath me, fingers manacling my wrists. He'd been faking. *Faking*. Oh, God, he'd never been in danger at all, had been in league with Dr. Frankenstein all along. How could I have been stupid enough to trust Leona? I needed air. I kicked, trying to blast my way to the surface, but Vincent held me back, fingers digging into my wrists, pulling me down, drowning me.

I kicked again, clawing, forgot myself and breathed in water, choked, fought harder, choked a second time, thrashing in a death struggle.

Whoever said drowning was a peaceful way to go obviously never tried it.

Someone clamped something over my mouth, and I breathed in air, heaving, choking on the water still in my lungs. I sucked in two thin breaths, enough to know that there wasn't a heck of a lot left, before Vincent pulled the mask away.

Fair enough. He needed oxygen, too.

So he wasn't on Dr. Frankenstein's side; he'd just mistaken me for Frankenstein in the dark, that was all.

But now we'd been under the water too long. Dr. Frankenstein would know I hadn't just dived in and come back up.

I groped in the water and found Vincent's arm. I touched it to his chest, then pointed.

Vincent showed his assent by swimming off in that direction.

I turned and swam the other way. I felt blind and very, very weak. It took effort to fight flotation and swim underwater for a distance. My wounded arm was useless, and my legs kicked mechanically without any of the strength I was accustomed to exerting. My lungs burned, craving air.

I broke the surface near the side of the pool, not quite touching the tiles. I could hear the steady slap, slap of the water filter nearby.

I let only my head show above the water, enough to breathe and unmuffle my ears. It was hard not to gasp in air. The urge to vomit overcame me, and I ducked below the surface to stifle the sound.

The thought of getting vomit on my face almost made me puke again, and I quickly pulled myself along the edge of the pool, still striving not to make a sound.

Safety lay in movement. Somewhere out there, either slowly cruising the pool or walking the perimeter, was Dr. Frankenstein, his treasure hunt turned into a manhunt.

I needed to get out of the pool, but I lacked the strength to haul myself out quietly.

My weakness frightened me. I wanted to cling to the side of the pool, but that was the most dangerous place right now. I made myself glide away while I still had the strength to keep my head above water. The shallow end would be easier for Dr. Frankenstein to search than the deep end, but I needed to be able to touch bottom. I took my best guess as to direction and headed down the middle of the pool, using a slow, slow sidestroke.

Slap, slap. Slap, slap. The water filter made the only sound. In the dark it was hard to believe that three other people shared the space with me—Vincent and me in the pool, Dr. Frankenstein and Mike on the tile deck.

Mike, where are you?

I tried to put my feet down and almost wept with relief when my toes touched bottom. A few more strokes and I stopped, listening.

A scuff, maybe. A small splash, impossible to judge the direction or guess whether it was friend or foe. Dr. Frankenstein had it easier that way. Everyone was his enemy.

Standing still, I began to feel very cold—shock from the bullet wound. I had to clench my teeth to keep them from chattering. *Please, Mike, if I've ever needed someone it's now.* I put one hand over my shoulder trying to stanch the flow of blood.

A small wave lapped at my chin. Something was moving toward me in the water. Vincent? I would soon need help to stay on my feet.

Ghostly currents of water caressed my skin. At the last instant I guessed what the currents meant and slipped beneath the surface, turning over into a dead man's float.

Water covered my ears, both muffling and intensifying sound. I stayed very, very still as Dr. Frankenstein slid through the water only a few feet away. I floated, drifting, and his hand grazed my foot.

I felt the start go through him, water being pushed into different shapes, as his hands grabbed me, found me limp and unresisting, dead. But Dr. Frankenstein was never one to take chances. He grabbed a handful of my wet hair and pressed the gun to my temple.

A loud splash from across the pool—Vincent getting out?—and Dr. Frankenstein fired at the sound.

I kicked his belly with all my strength, which was not much, pushed myself underwater, and swam farther into the shallow end, scraping my arms on the rough cement.

Behind me Dr. Frankenstein swore and fired again—must be an old gun with real bullets, to be so loud. Were you fast enough, Vincent, or did he hit you, too?

Disjointed thoughts. I clung to the side of the pool—it was shallow enough here to kneel— only gradually becoming aware that Dr. Frankenstein was splashing far too much, firing too wildly.

My heart lurched inside me. Mike. He had followed Dr. Frankenstein into the water and jumped him. They were fighting for the gun now.

I could do nothing but cling to the side of the pool, my strength spent, blood washing out of me in an imagined torrent. I was still clinging when the victor sloshed toward me. I was helpless prey if it proved to be Dr. Frankenstein. If Mike was dead, I hardly cared.

A hand touched me, and I slipped out of reach, down into the water's embrace.

CHAPTER

19

"ANGEL. Angel, you have to wake up," Mike whispered urgently.

I opened my eyes, but the pool remained in darkness. I could barely make out Mike's face, scant inches from mine. I was wrapped up in a blanket and Mike's arms. Vincent stood nearby.

"Dr. Frankenstein?" I croaked.

"Dead. The gun . . ." Mike didn't say any more. He didn't need to.

"You saved my life," I reminded him. "Vincent's, too."

Mike ignored my words. "You've been shot. You fainted. How are you feeling?"

"Pretty lousy." I coughed weakly, aware of a burning streak in my shoulder where the bullet had torn through.

"Can you go back in the water?" Vincent asked bluntly.

I understood at once. He was asking me to

play dead for the cameras. "Yes." I had to; there was no choice.

"No," Mike said. "I don't think she should. She's in shock already. She could drown."

"It's our only chance to avoid Dr. Frankenstein's customers," Vincent argued. "Believe me, you don't want to work for them."

His voice made me shudder. Or maybe it was the shock. "Vincent won't talk about what they made him do," Leona had said, "but I know it was bad."

I had no desire to find out for myself how bad it could be. "I can do it."

"It's a delaying tactic at best. The customers will find out eventually what happened, and we don't even know that Leona understands our scheme," Mike protested.

"You said she made a signal like taking a photograph. She'll be there." Vincent was confident of his sister's capability.

I was confident that Leona had understood—but not confident that she was ready and waiting in whatever communications room the live feed to Dr. Frankenstein's customers was passing through. Her leg was broken and she'd been unconscious, possibly concussed, when we found her.

"I can do it," I repeated, fighting not to shiver.

Mike snarled something but didn't argue anymore. He and Vincent began moving the players into place. They posed Dr. Frankenstein's body in a chair with his eyes open and the bullet hole in his heart covered by his jacket.

They faked up a lifesaving dummy to play the part of Vincent, down at the bottom of the pool, chained to the empty oxygen tank. I was next.

Sliding down into the water felt like going into a glacier-fed stream. I was so cold. . . .

Mike made me take a small ball to use as a flotation device. He towed me out to a spot in the deep end not far from the diving board, since I was too weak to swim on my own. Then he swam out to his own spot, closer to the shallow end. Vincent was responsible for the lights. I closed my eyes and hung on to the ball, drifting.

Countdown. Five, four, three, two, one. I was facedown in the water when the lights came on. I held my breath for as long as I could, until my head started to spin and I started to lose my grip on the ball, until I couldn't bear it, plus five seconds more.

It was the best I could do. I came up gasping for air.

We had to trust that the shot of three bodies would make Dr. Frankenstein's customers believe us dead and Leona incapacitated—at least for a while. We had to trust that Leona had done her job, cutting the transmission at the right moment.

Mike quickly swam over to me and helped me out of the pool, swaddling me in blankets a second time. "Vincent's gone to get the first aid kit. Take this." Mike passed me a can of Orange Crush. I swallowed down the sweet, sticky beverage gladly. I needed to replace some of the fluid I had lost.

Vincent showed up with the kit and quickly got down to business. "I'm going to be a doctor," he told me, gently probing the wound. "I've been reading books this last month. Trust me."

I gritted my teeth and bore the pain. I refused to faint even when he sterilized the wound.

"There," Vincent said, taping the last gauze pad firmly in place. "If you don't get a fever, you should be able to avoid a trip to the hospital."

That was an important point. Although the riot had broken the back of the Renaissance Project, I wanted to blend into society quietly, not announce myself to radical groups—or to world powers looking for hot deals on super-spies.

"I won't get a fever," I said positively.

Mike raised an eyebrow.

I smiled an angel's incandescent smile. "Renaissance genes. We don't get sick as often as *sapiens* either, haven't you noticed?"

"Sorry I tried to drown you earlier," Vincent said with his usual directness. "I thought you were Frankenstein, come to cut loose the air tanks."

"I would have done the same." I was feeling generous.

Mike scavenged up another car, and the three of us drove back to the old folks' home. I waited in the car, exhausted, while Mike and Vincent carried Leona out.

Her face was pale and harsh with pain as they laid her on the backseat of the car. To distract her on the brief drive to the deserted hospital I asked her if she'd gotten enough videotape of us playing dead for the cameras.

"Yes," Leona said tersely.

"She did better than that," Vincent said, unmistakable pride in his voice. "Tell her."

"It was nothing." Leona shifted restlessly. "I found some software that let me make a loop of the videotape of darkness and splashing sounds. I transmitted that while I fixed the inconsistencies of the death shot. I inserted old footage of Dr. Frankenstein coming into the pool room before sitting in the chair where you left him so it didn't appear as if the lights came on by magic. Then I added a voice-over spliced together from his computer message announcing himself the winner of the *sapiens* versus *renascentia* battle and saying he would soon return to his office and kill me."

"That doesn't sound like 'nothing' to me," I said, impressed.

Leona shrugged. "His customers will still figure it out. We're only buying time. You two should go. You're wasting time here."

"Not until your leg is set," I said firmly.

We reached the hospital, and, as promised, Mike helped Vincent set Leona's leg and put a cast on it. Vincent frowned at the plaster-dipped bandages. "They must have found a better way to do this by now."

His words sobered me. When we left Chinchaga we would be jumping feet first into the next century.

"Where do you guys plan to go now that you're free?" I asked Vincent and Leona.

Vincent and Leona exchanged glances.

"It's okay," I said, sensing their distrust. "You don't have to tell me."

Vincent shook his head. "No, it's all right. We're going to contact the underground movement. Catherine promised she'd help us look for Erin Reinders and my baby."

"What about you two? You're welcome to come with us," Leona said unexpectedly, considering our past clashes.

I didn't need to look at Mike to know his answer. "No, thanks." That seemed too abrupt, so I added, "We want to make our own way, as ourselves, not as Renaissance children." I didn't know what we would do or what we would become, but I knew I wanted to be judged for Angel Eastland's mistakes, not for the faults and virtues of the Renaissance subspecies.

Leona nodded. She seemed to understand. "Good luck, then."

Formally, Mike and I shook their hands and left. I wished Leona and Vincent success in their search, but I would not miss either of them.

I would, however, miss my parents and Wendy and Carl. Once things became safer, I promised myself I would find a way to meet them again, under a different name and with colored contact lenses to disguise my violet eyes.

"Are you ready?" Mike asked softly as we walked past the town boundary, crossing from 1987 into the future in one step.

I had the same doubts that Mike had, the

same doubts any human being would feel when entering a new world. I also had the same hopes. "I'm ready."

Mike kissed me softly. We would make it. I knew it.

The newshounds found Dr. Frankenstein's body floating in the pool and made a big ruckus over the note they found in a Ziploc bag pinned to the body:

> We would rather be your friends
> than your enemies.
> Don't start a war you can't win.

About the Author

NICOLE LUIKEN was born May 25, 1971. She grew up on a farm in northern Alberta (latitude 57° N). She wrote her first novel at age thirteen (it was summer holidays and there was nothing else to do). She is the author of three young adult novels (*Unlocking the Doors, The Catalyst,* and *Escape to Overworld*) and one adult thriller (*Running on Instinct*). She lives in Edmonton, Alberta, with her husband, Aaron Humphrey, and young son, Simon, and is currently working on a sequel to *Violet Eyes*. It is physically impossible for her to go without writing for more than three days in a row.

... A GIRL BORN WITHOUT THE FEAR GENE

FEARLESS™

A SERIES BY
FRANCINE PASCAL

FROM POCKET PULSE
PUBLISHED BY POCKET BOOKS

3029